Little White Lies and Butterflies

Suzie Tullett

Print ISBN 978-1-912175-57-4

Also By Suzie Tullett

The Trouble With Words

Praise for The Trouble With Words:

"*Tullett has a very descriptive, vivid writing style and discusses the characters feelings and emotional outlook quite a bit. It was really heartfelt and touching, a truly fun read.*"
Amy Sullivan - Novelgossip

"*Suzie Tullett has a way with words that will have you laughing one minute and crying the next. She engages her readers, taking them on an emotional journey with a cast of characters who felt like friends by the end.*"
Joanne Robertson - My Chestnut Reading Tree

"*I cannot find the words to tell you exactly how much I loved this book! The storyline is unique, the characters are complex and original, and the heart-warming factor is off the Richter scale.*"
Kaisha Holloway - The Writing Garnet

"*The Trouble With Words is a well crafted read that encompasses some very heavy topics but allows the reader to see the positive side as well.*"
Alison Daughtrey-Drew - Ali - The Dragon Slayer

"*The novel has its ups and downs emotionally and whilst I knew that the story had to have an ending, I really didn't want get to that part, it really was the heart-warming romantic comedy that it was billed to be and I loved how I felt when reading it...*"
Donna Maguire - Donnas Book Blog

"*The Trouble With Words made me pretty emotional but also left me with a wonderful sense of hope that was just perfect. This story brings so much to the reader engaging characters, an emotional pull and a lovely heart warming feeling.*"

Rachel Broughton - Rae Reads

For Adam, who never fails to make me smile.

CHAPTER ONE

From outside the dance circle, you sing lots of songs.

'That's it!' I announced, having just landed at Mum and Dad's house for our customary Sunday lunch gathering. 'My life as I know it is officially over!'

I paused, waiting for that all important condoling response. Daft enough to expect at least a modicum of sympathy from within the bosom of my family, I quickly realised I should've known better. The Livingstons didn't do compassion.

Instead, Mum appeared with a mass of cutlery, her arm outstretched as she thrust it my way. 'If you wouldn't mind,' she said, pointing me in the direction of the dining room table.

Mum headed back into the kitchen, leaving me no choice but to get on with it. However, as I spotted Dad already seated and eager to eat, I did suppose the woman needed all the help she could get. Certain members of our family had always preferred a more observational role when it came to mucking in with the household chores; Dad was a prime example of this.

'Oh, yes,' I continued, regardless. 'My dreams have finally been crushed, once and for all.'

I began laying the table, sucking myself in as I squeezed behind my somewhat unaccommodating father, a man more concerned about his belly's grumblings than those of his beloved offspring.

'Leaving me no choice but to think about joining a convent,' I carried on. 'Where I shall, no doubt, remain for the rest of my days.'

'Things didn't go too well, then?' asked Mum, suddenly re-emerging with a stack of plates, eager to get the task at hand done and dusted.

Not that I minded her hurrying me along in my moment of distress. After all, everyone knew it paid dividends to have everything organised and in place before brother number one, Steve, and his wife, Jill, arrived with their not so adorable kids in tow. Although, to be fair, it wasn't so much my sullen fifteen-year-old niece who created cause for concern – texting, tweeting Tammy, as I liked to refer to her – but more my yet to be diagnosed ADHD suffering little nephews, eight-year-old twins Luke and Johnny.

'The trouble with you, Lydia,' Dad joined in, although just to clarify, by that I mean with the conversation and not the workload, 'is you're far too picky.'

I watched him fold his arms as if he'd just imparted some piece of crucial advice. *Obviously, a chap who wants nothing but the best for his one and only daughter.* Although at the same time, I did have to acknowledge he wasn't exactly the first person to suggest I might be setting my sights a little higher than was good for me. Unrealistic, for want of a better word.

'Too ugly, you mean,' corrected a rather bedraggled Pete, brother number two, as he appeared in the doorway – a man who needed to choose his words a little more carefully in my view, especially when I still had a couple of knives in my hand.

'Do the words pot, kettle and black mean anything to you?' I asked.

He plonked himself down at the table and, yet again, I found myself understanding why his long-suffering girlfriend had finally decided to kick him to the kerb, sending both him and his belongings back home to Mummy.

'If you must know,' I said, getting back to the more important issue under discussion. 'This one met *all* the necessary criteria. He even asked if he could see me again.'

Mum suddenly stopped what she was doing. 'So, what's the problem, then?'

She had spent years listening to me recount the events of one disastrous date after another, all the while harping on about not settling for second best and bagging my perfect man by the time I hit thirty, so I understood her surprise. The way I'd gone on I should've been chomping at the bit to book the church for the wedding by now, or at least be sending the invitations out for the engagement party.

'Well, I can't be sure,' I ventured. 'But I think this one had some sort of medical condition.'

'Ha!' scoffed Pete. 'I knew it. He was blind, wasn't he? Had to be, to be seen out in public with you.'

I forced myself to put the last of the knives down. 'No. Not exactly.'

Mum handed me half her pile of plates.

'What do you mean? Not exactly?' Dad laughed, as usual failing to take my quest at all seriously.

'It wasn't so much he couldn't see,' I said. 'But more that he didn't blink.'

I ignored Pete's sniggering.

'And did you ask him about it?' enquired Mum. 'It might've been curable.'

'No, I didn't!' I replied. 'Just because he wasn't *The One* doesn't mean I'd want to hurt the guy's feelings.

'Besides, that's not the point, is it?' I continued. 'If I start making concessions now, just because time's running out, all the other naff dates will have been for nothing. And in that case, I may as well have just married a fool like *him* from the off,' I indicated to my not-so-darling brother, 'and have been done with it years ago.'

Mum rolled her eyes, probably picturing me as an ageing spinster for the umpteenth time, spending my twilight years with nothing but a room full of cats for company. 'I blame all those silly books you read,' she said. 'Putting ideas into young girls' heads like they do. They're just not realistic.'

'I'll tell you what's not realistic,' I replied. 'Women who think they can have it all.'

Dad threw his head back and groaned. 'Here we go again,' he said, failing to realise he'd been proving my point since the day I was born.

'Just look at you, Mum – you work all the hours God sends, then come home and run around after these two, because heaven forbid they should have to do something for themselves.'

'There's nothing wrong with a woman having a career, Lydia,' she replied.

'No, there isn't. And there's nothing wrong with having a family either. As for having both—despite what everyone preaches, what everyone's always preached, you of all people know it isn't everything it's cracked up to be.'

Mum, Dad, and Pete stared at me like I'd lost the plot, while I looked from the crockery in Mum's hands to the crockery in mine.

Still, in my experience it didn't matter how often I tried to explain. When it came to the career versus family argument I knew they'd never be able to understand why, well into the twenty-first century, I'd find it acceptable to choose one over the other. Why I'd choose domesticity over a job.

Then again, thinking back to the couple of hours wasted on the latest, and as it turned out blinkingly challenged, conjugal contender, I had to admit this was something even I was beginning to question.

'Not that I suppose it matters now, anyway,' I reluctantly conceded. 'Which is why you'll all be pleased to know I've finally decided to take stock.'

The relief on Mum's face was immeasurable, no doubt because she was glad to hear her next set of grandchildren weren't going to be of the feline kind, after all. 'Well that's something, I suppose,' she said.

'Yes, well, before you all go and get your hopes up too much, just because I'm abandoning my mission doesn't mean I'm about to enrol on some course and get myself a proper job, as you lot call it! No, siree. Instead, I'm going to banish myself to a distant land and head off into the wild blue yonder.' I threw my arm out in a dramatic gesture. 'A place where I can reassess my situation and decide where to go from here.'

'I knew it was too good to be true,' said Dad, obviously viewing my assertion as another of '*those melodramatic tendencies*' he'd always thought me prone to.

'What do you mean?' asked Mum. 'Take yourself off into the wild blue yonder?'

I got back to laying the table. 'Well, if I'm not going to use my wedding fund for an actual wedding,' I explained, 'I might as well put it to some other good use. And I think a bit of time and space away from everything is just what I need right now.'

'And when do you plan on going?'

'As soon as…'

'But you can't,' interrupted Mum. 'What about your birthday? I've already ordered the cake.'

'I've decided I'm not celebrating it this year,' I replied. 'Being thirty and still single isn't exactly something I want to shout from the rooftops, is it? Not after everything I've been through.'

'Now she really has lost her marbles,' said Dad.

'That's if she ever had any to begin with,' said Pete.

CHAPTER TWO

A cassock doesn't make someone a priest.

*N*ow *I know why they call these things Dolphins,* I thought, the boat rather energetically bouncing up and down as it cut through the water's surface. *Although it has to be said that real dolphins are a lot more graceful. And probably not quite as fast!*

With my hair blowing about all over the place and my beloved Beckhamesque sunglasses about to fly off my face at any given moment, I knew any attempts at appearing the consummate traveller were fast disappearing. And, fighting to keep my bum on the bench, convinced that I, too, would be tossed overboard if I dared release my grip in the slightest, I began to question why I'd seen fit to choose a deck seat in the first place. In fact, I began to ask what I was doing on the boat at all.

Determined not to lose control altogether, I willed myself to at least try and enjoy the ride and, with the boat leaving Kos well and truly behind in favour of its neighbouring Kalymnos, I endeavoured to take in the rest of my surroundings.

I mean, it isn't every day you get to see a sight like this, is it?

I stared out at the largest expanse of Brandeis blue I'd ever seen, under the most glorious of Mediterranean sunshine, and even I had to admit the energetic crossing was *sort* of worth the discomfort. But as the vessel rose to the challenge of yet another swell of surf, I found it a struggle to remain quite so positive. *I just wish I wasn't bobbing up and down quite as much. So, I could actually enjoy it.*

It was my first time in the Dodecanese and my Greek geography knowledge was strictly limited to some of the larger islands like Corfu and Zante; up until recently, I'd never actually heard of Kalymnos, let alone of its rocky, rugged landscape. But into the travel agency I'd gone, armed with my long list of requirements for that perfect exile experience and, a few taps on her computer later, this was the little slice of paradise the agent had come up with.

I only hope the place lives up to its reputation, I thought, remembering the woman's somewhat poetic description of what was to become my home for the next few weeks. Although as I looked about at my fellow passengers, also recalling her telling me about its popularity among the world's climbing fraternity, I doubted if she'd really had a clue as to what she'd been talking about. This one aspect of reality was already failing to meet expectations.

She obviously has an overactive imagination, I complained inwardly, while continuing to observe the rucksack- and kit-carrying individuals around me. Because instead of the host of handsome, muscular, athletic types I had hoped to feast my eyes upon, I couldn't have come face to face with a scruffier group of crag rats if I'd tried. *Wide-leg sweatpants are horrific at the best of times, but wearing them a couple of inches too short is just scandalous.*

And what was it with the dreadlocks and Jesus sandals? But as if things couldn't get any worse, any disenchantment I felt soon turned into a sense of nausea, all courtesy of the array of tighter than necessary leggings on display. After all, these garments aren't just offensive per se; when it comes to a man's particular body parts, surely an air of mystery needs to be maintained?

I realised my observations hadn't gone unnoticed when I spotted one of the climbers giving me the glad eye. Not that this one appeared as extreme as all the others, I noted. This chap preferred to wear knee-length combats and a simple T-shirt, rather than one of the more grotesque outfits on view. If I ignored the overgrown, sun-kissed hair and blocked out the not-so-designer stubble, he probably wasn't all *that* bad looking underneath. Nevertheless, he still wasn't my type; although, if experience was anything to go by, I couldn't be certain my type even existed.

If he does, he most certainly isn't among this lot. I took another look at the inferior gene pool around me. Not that you're here to think about any of that anyway.

I turned away, determined to dismiss all images of bulging Lycra-covered crotches completely from my mind. Ready to embrace what lay ahead as the content, happily single woman I was clearly destined to be, I returned my attention to the rest of my surroundings, excited to see that we were fast approaching Kalymnos.

As the boat entered the harbour of Pothia, it struck me just how Venetian the island looked as opposed to anything Greek and, whereas I'd anticipated seeing a mass of traditional blue and white when it came to the architecture, much to my surprise, I found myself taking in a multitude of terracotta, peaches and yellows. Thinking back to the little bit of googling I had managed to squeeze in before my departure, I recollected something about it being under Italian rule up until as late as 1947 and so I guessed a certain influence was hardly surprising.

Everyone around me suddenly sprang to their feet and, all at once, began heading down to the holding area. However, it wasn't a large boat to begin with and, with the sudden uneven weight distribution, I started to feel a slight panic. As far as I was concerned, the other passengers obviously knew something I didn't and watching them all clamour to undertake a mass exodus the second we finally docked, I quickly came to the conclusion that I'd better join them in their fight for dry land. Rising to my feet, I told myself if this craft was going to go down, I had no intention of going down with it and so I pushed and shoved my way down the steps and along the gangplank with the rest of them, until my feet hit terra firma.

Wrestling with my mammoth suitcase, I battled my way through the crowds and over to one of the waiting taxis.

'Your first time here?' asked the driver, trying not to grimace too much as he windlassed my luggage into the boot.

I realised it was the suitcase that had given me away. The more seasoned visitors all had backpacks.

'So where to?' he asked.

I dug my booking sheet out of my bag, while he took his position behind the wheel.

'Fatolitis in Massouri,' I said and, just glad to be leaving all that confused hustle and bustle behind me, I heaved a great big sigh of relief. At last, my well-earned sabbatical could start for real.

We made our way over to the north side of the island, climbing steadily up through villages with names like Xora and Elies. Being a newbie visitor, I considered them all of interest in their own right, although the more we journeyed, the more I noticed a distinct lack of tourism on display. In fact, there wasn't much of anything taking place at all, apart from people going about their everyday lives in pretty much the same way they would at home – only here, they could do it in the sunshine. However, there were lots of old men sitting in cafés, drinking coffee and smoking— another reminder that it was a good job I'd decided to put my manhunt on hold *before* I actually got there, otherwise I'd now be doubly disappointed.

We turned the bend that signalled our eventual descent and I immediately shot forward in my seat. *Now this is more like it,* I thought, God's honest beauty of Kalymnos finally hitting me in the face. 'Wow!' I said, mesmerized. 'It's like something out of *Jason and the Argonauts!*'

I began rooting in my bag for my camera. 'Can we stop for a minute?' I asked, mid-search, 'so I can get one for the album?'

The driver did as I asked and pulled over, enabling me to jump out and make the most of our vantage point as I click-clicked away, taking one photograph after another. But after a moment I paused to really absorb the sight before me, the harsh barrenness of the mountainous Kalymnian shoreline proudly rising up from the bluest of oceans almost taking my breath away.

'Magnificent!' I said, staring out at a spectacle more reminiscent of Ancient Greece than any modern-day vista I'd ever seen before. I envisaged the great Poseidon suddenly heaving himself up out of the waters, only to hoist the smaller island opposite off its anchor in an angry god-like display.

'That's Talendos,' explained the driver, as if reading my mind.

'It's incredible,' I replied, still gazing out to sea.

The driver started his engine signalling it was time to set off again, leaving me no choice but to climb back into the car.

'I think I'm going to enjoy my time here,' I said, as we began following the somewhat windy road down towards our destination.

We came to a standstill outside Fatolitis and my Kalymnian reverie came to an abrupt end. 'There must be some mistake,' I said, bolting upright.

'No, no mistake,' said the driver. 'This is Fatolitis.'

I stared out of the window. 'But it's a bar!' I protested.

Yet again, I tried to remember the travel agent's words, knowing full well I wouldn't have booked this trip if she'd told me about this. If I'd wanted to spend my holiday listening to vacationing lager louts all hell-bent on swilling alcohol and singing the latest in dance anthems until the early hours of the morning, I'd have blooming well gone to Benidorm, for goodness sake. A fact that was clearly of no concern to anyone but me, I realised – at least, it wasn't if the way this guy was out of the car and dumping my suitcase on the roadside was anything to go by.

I followed him to the back of the vehicle. 'But it's a bar,' I repeated, once more to no avail.

'Fifteen euros,' he simply said, hand out at the ready.

I took my purse out of my bag and handed the money over, leaving him free to head off in search of his next fare and me just standing there like a lemon watching him go.

Now what was I to do?

I glanced up at what was evidently to be my apartment directly above the bar, before returning my attention back to the business below, all the while trying to reassure myself it wasn't that bad as far as accommodation went. Rather than an all-night rock and roll venue, with its welcoming vine-covered seating area and convivial atmosphere, it seemed more of a place in which to escape the heat of the midday sun or, indeed, unwind after a hard day's climbing.

'Please, no! Not climbing,' I lamented.

Doing my utmost to resist the stretch material flashbacks, I began to really take in the not-so-subtle clues as to the bar's predominant clientele. Clues like numerous posters depicting rocky scenes adorning the walls, a cluster of climbing shoes dangling by the entrance, and, much to my horror, a climbing rope hanging like some sort of noose from the otherwise pretty liana.

'Fan-bloody-tastic!'

An older, well-built gentleman caught my eye when he suddenly appeared from out back—thankfully snapping me out of my nightmare.

'You must be Lydia,' he said, wearing the friendliest of smiles and speaking in the most endearing of broken English accents.

'Mr Fatolitis?' I cautiously confirmed, at the same time stepping forward to return his greeting.

He completely ignored my outstretched palm and my eyes widened when he instead firmly grabbed me by the shoulders and planted his lips onto either side of my face.

'Oh,' I said, bouncing off his rather rotund midriff. 'I wasn't expecting that.' Although I should've known a simple handshake wasn't the Mediterranean way of doing things, and took a moment to recover. Compared to people in the UK, the southern Europeans had always been a passionate lot.

My host proffered a dismissive wave of his hand. He clearly didn't have any time for the British stiff upper lip and, rather than pander to my awkwardness, he actually appeared quite amused by it. 'Please,' he said. 'I'm Efthimeos.'

He reverted back to his mother tongue, calling out in the direction from which he'd just come, and the rest of the family matched his enthusiasm as they raced out to meet me.

'This is Maria,' my host explained, ushering the first of the trio forward. 'My wife.'

She garbled something in Greek and I soon found myself on the receiving end of yet another wholehearted bear hug. Just like her husband, Maria also modelled a fuller figure, except in her case it wasn't just around the middle. I flushed red, squashed against the biggest pair of boobs I'd ever seen let alone been that close to. Although she obviously didn't have an issue with personal space, I most certainly did.

'Welcome,' she said at last, letting me go.

Her generous smile persisted, but something in her eyes told me that that was probably it as far as her English went and, considering I didn't speak a word of Greek to help make up the deficit, I thought it safer to just keep things simple. 'Thank you,' I replied, meeting her smile with one of my own.

Efthimeos indicated to the next in line. 'And this is Katerina,' he said. 'My daughter.'

A pretty young woman, who clearly took after her mother in the big breast department, I noticed her immediately looking me up and down.

As if I didn't feel self-conscious enough already.

'You are here alone?' she asked. 'You have no friends?'

Her directness caught me off guard; such candour being something I'd never quite experienced before, I didn't really know how to respond.

'Worse, you have no man?' she added.

I inwardly cringed; Katerina's mastery of English linguistics sounding a bit *too* good for my liking—an opinion that extended to her body language. The accompanying look of pity in her eyes was sufficiently recognisable, even without the dramatic hand up to the chest gesture. A gesture I could have more than done without, especially when my single status was a sore enough subject to begin with.

'Erm, no,' I replied, hoping to sound a lot more confident, easy and breezy on the matter than I actually felt. 'It's just me, I'm afraid.'

She shook her head at what she clearly thought my utter misfortune. 'I am so lucky,' she crooned, taking a quick admiring glance at herself in the nearest available reflective surface.

Who is this girl? I secretly asked.

Much to my relief Efthimeos decided to move on. 'And finally,' he said. 'This is Yiannis, my son.'

Our eyes met and instantly Katerina's words disappeared.

Now this is more like it. My spirits suddenly lifted at the sight of the vision of loveliness before me. It was all I could do to stop myself from giggling, and I tried to ignore the intensifying fluttering in my abdomen. When he leaned forward and his lips met my cheeks, his embrace was a lot more enjoyable than it should have been, particularly as Yiannis looked even younger than his sister. Although, in my defence, the guy also looked like Greece's answer to Ricky Martin, and, with a bit of luck on my part, would be quite a lot straighter.

I wondered if, at almost thirty, I was old enough to be deemed a Cougar. The 'older woman with a younger man' syndrome was all the rage these days. *Not that you should be thinking about members of the opposite sex that way, anyway.* I was forced to remind myself that this trip was meant to be about anything but what did and didn't constitute my perfect man.

Still, I conceded. *I don't suppose there's any harm in just looking.* And rather than deny myself the pleasure altogether, I most certainly did look.

'Don't listen to her,' he said, rolling his eyes at his sister while speaking in the most heavenly of voices. I almost swooned. 'She's just showing off. She's getting married in a couple of weeks and that's her way of letting everyone know.'

His words stung like a slap in the face, immediately bringing me back to my senses.

'Sorry?' I asked. 'Did you just say she's getting married?'

He nodded.

'As in there's going to be a wedding?'

'Yiannis,' Efthimeos interrupted, at the same time indicating to my luggage. 'Could you show Lydia to her room?'

'No problem,' he replied. 'And yes,' he said to me, 'there is to be a wedding.'

I took in his muscular frame as he heaved my suitcase up onto his shoulder with ease, but the magic was gone.

So, let me get this straight, I thought, struggling to get my head around what I'd just heard. *I travel all this way to distance myself from all things bride and groom, only to find there's a wedding about to take place right under my nose?*

'Great!' I muttered, as I, at last, began following Yiannis' footsteps. 'That's all I blooming well need!'

CHAPTER THREE

The woman who doesn't wish to bake bread, spends five days sifting the flour.

I threw open the shutters and looked out to sea, taking a moment to enjoy the warm morning breeze.

I could definitely get used to this. I spotted a little fishing boat as it chug-chugged its way back to shore, all the while being mobbed by a flock of hungry seagulls. 'Nope, you certainly don't get views like this where I come from.'

But, knowing me, even if I did have something nicer than a row of terraces to look out on back in Lancashire, I realised I probably wouldn't take the time to actually enjoy it. In the real world, life consisted of work, work, work and yet more work in one form or another, leaving little or no time for anything else. Not that my job in the local café was particularly arduous, I acknowledged. That simply involved a lot of smiling and taking orders on account of my inability to cook. But still, it did take up the majority of my week, and had done since I left college. Not that I'd intended on being a waitress for quite that long. I had thought I'd be well into wedded bliss by the time I hit my twenties. I was supposed to have kids by now.

College... I sighed. Where had the years gone?

I tried to work out where all my time went, now adding the ritual Sunday lunch at Mum and Dad's into my schedule. A chore in itself that took up more or less a full day thanks to my not-very-droll brothers and not-so-adorable little nephews. I could picture myself batting off the insults, mediating the squabbles, and tackling the mountain of washing up that had been amassed once everyone had finished stuffing their faces. Of course, all I really wanted to do was spend the last day of the week taking my time over the morning papers, nipping down to my local pub for a leisurely afternoon or generally just vegging out in my own home—something Mum wouldn't hear a word of.

On top of all that, I had to factor in all the hours I physically spent on my manhunt—and those didn't just include the unsuitable dates with a long list of equally unsuitable men. 'And all for what?' I sighed, for the first time fully conceding just how crappy my existence had been up until now. 'For absolutely nothing…'

I wondered if I should've spent more time just standing and staring like this. If I had, things might've turned out differently. 'Still, at least you've made the decision to work on changing things now,' I said, trying not to be too hard on myself. 'Surely late's got to be better than never.' What changes had I planned to make exactly, or, indeed, how was I going to go about making them? There were clearly things I still needed to figure out. But on the plus side, I knew my life was no longer going to revolve around men. Oh no, as far as I was concerned, hadn't I wasted enough time and energy on the not-so-fair sex already?

Dragging myself away from the window and its fabulous view, I took in the room around me. Its whitewashed walls and modest cream furniture contrasted beautifully with the odd accent of crimson here and there; the whole ensemble was quite stunning in its simplicity. *Why can't life be like this? Free of any unnecessary clutter, no pretentions, effortless yet perfect?* Then I laughed, the cynic inside me recognising it was all just an illusion anyway; that creating such a sense of simplicity in truth took a whole lot of work—something I knew all about. But there was no point in complaining, what was done was done and, pulling myself together, I began getting my bag ready for a day's relaxation at the beach—a great place to spend some thinking time.

'Suncream… check! Towel… check! Book… check!'

My ears pricked as the chattering of the Fatolitis family made its way up to my room. *No doubt getting ready for their own day ahead.* I tried to work out where one word ended and the next one began but, without any knowledge of Greek, their conversation to me sounded more like a string of garbled syllables rather than any actual exchange. 'Maybe you should try and learn a bit,' I said to myself, thinking a few key phrases might be useful during my stay. *Learning a new language could be fun and if listening to them is anything to go by, it'll most certainly be a challenge.* And I felt sure if I asked, the family would be only too happy to help; after all, they'd proven themselves to be so utterly accommodating already, having spent most of the previous night running up and down the steps making sure I had everything I needed and knew where everything was. 'Mind you, that's probably because they felt sorry for me more than anything else,' I decided. 'Despite it being the twenty-first century, a woman forced to go on holiday on her own and all that.'

Deep down, I didn't really mind their sympathy as such. It was comforting to think both their little taverna and their kindness might provide me with something of a home from home—especially when in many ways this somewhat frenetic Greek family very much reminded me of my own nearest and dearest. *Ooh, while it's on my mind, I still need to call home.*

I grabbed a pen to make a note so I wouldn't forget, scribbling down the reminder with a great big star next to it signifying its importance and telling myself that I should really make a point of ringing Mum and Dad as soon as possible. I knew if I didn't, the Livingstons would only start panicking and fussing just as much as the Fatolitis had been.

'Not that comparing family traits is going to get you to the beach any time soon,' I reproached myself, throwing the last of my bits and bobs into my bag before zipping it shut ready for the off.

Then, after a quick glance around to make sure I did, in fact, have everything I needed, I finally headed out.

The stroll down to the village square was divine—the sun on my skin, the gentle breeze floating on the air and best of all no climbers around, meaning my eyes could roam at will without being subject to any unpleasantries in stretchy material. What could be better? I squinted, attempting to focus on the mountainside, fathoming they must all still be hanging off one of the many rock faces around. Free from distractions, I was able to take in the more beautiful aspects of the environment, pleased to note the intense cerise of the bougainvillea set against the bluest of cloudless skies and the pretty, pastel-painted houses that were more reminiscent of Italy than of Greece.

I looked out to Talendos, rising out of the water like some craggy mini volcano, thinking it would be nice to spend some time over there as well during my stay. Not that there appeared to be much going on; I could only spot one little community and a stretch of sand. Plenty enough for little old me, though, and as it couldn't be more than a ten-minute boat ride away, surely there had to be some sort of commuting service running. At least, I hoped there was a service; it looked like such a delightful little place … Very romantic!

My stomach sank, romantic being the operative word. Of course, I wouldn't be going over! It was obviously a place you visited with that special someone, not on your own like some saddo Billy No Mates. I sighed. Maybe Dad had been right all along. Maybe I had been too picky when it came to men? But ever since I could read, I'd always craved my very own fairy-tale ending, my very own Prince Charming... and was I *really* so wrong for that?

'Now you're just being silly,' I told myself. 'Of course you're not wrong.' After all, just because the men *I* knew didn't live up to the title didn't mean he wasn't out there somewhere.

Although none of this really mattered anymore, I realised, not now I'd given up the search. And besides, being in Greece as a singleton had got to be better than being there with a frog? 'No matter what Dad thinks.' Although in my view, 'frog' probably wasn't the right description for some of the men I'd been on dates with. Toad? Yes, maybe. Snake? Quite possibly! But as I thought back to my most recent dating disasters I couldn't be sure these particular amphibians were very apt either. I mean, didn't toads and snakes blink?

I started the descent down the steps to the beach. *It's always the parents' fault anyway,* I thought, more than happy to lay the blame for my storybook ideals firmly on Mum and Dad's shoulders. 'When it comes to Dad, as lovely as he can be at times, he isn't exactly a prime example of the so-called new man—mentally, physically, or otherwise!' Never in his life would he have worked a hundred plus hours a week, come home specially to bath his kids, even when they were still tots, and then clean the bathroom, but only after he'd tucked them into bed... and all before preparing the healthiest of suppers for his dearest wife, the very same woman he planned to make wonderful love to—once he'd stacked the dishwasher and carried her upstairs to bed, that is.

Whereas over the years, apart from the carrying my father up to the bedroom bit, thank you very much, I'd had to watch my mum struggle to do most, if not all of these things. When what she really should've done is insist on more help from her other half and, if he refused, to blooming well put her foot down. With role models like these, is it any wonder I strove for something different?

Unfortunately for me, though, it was a bit like pondering over the chicken and the egg, only in my case, it was a question of which came first, the fact or the fiction? The *fact* that this new man clearly didn't exist no matter what the commentators of my youth said, at least that was the message in every household I'd ever known. Or the *fiction* I'd always escaped into, which unwittingly reinforced all the hype that somewhere out there he really did exist after all?

Then again, I supposed it was still me who'd made the decision to choose a family over a career, regardless of who was to blame for my worldly outlook—even if it hadn't panned out quite the way I'd expected.

Finally reaching the bottom step, I looked out at the deserted sand before me, spotting lots of empty sunbeds but not a single person in sight to enjoy them. 'A beachside reflection of my empty existence,' I lamented, letting out a somewhat theatrical sigh.

A light bulb went on in my head. 'Maybe that's it?' A glimmer of something positive suddenly lit on the horizon. 'People are always saying I have a flair for the dramatic. Maybe I could become an actress?' I decided to put my thespian skills to the test, opting for a more Shakespearian style. 'Lydia Livingston,' I theatrically proclaimed, 'this golden expanse is merely the blank canvas of your life... Now go!' I swept my arm out for effect. 'Do with it what you will!'

Not bad, even if I did say so myself.

I glanced around, trying to decide on the perfect spot. Not too far from the water for when I needed a paddle, I fancied, and not too far from the bar for when I needed a drink. Opting for a sunbed somewhere between the two, I set up my stall and began slapping on the suncream. *Oh yes, this is the life.* At last I was ready to lie back and soak up the sunrays. However, the idyll wouldn't have been complete without a bit of Jane Austen in the picture. I picked up my book, intending on getting through at least a couple of chapters before breaking off for lunch.

A throng of unfamiliar voices tried to work their way into my head, but my sleepy brain had different ideas and refused to acknowledge them. However, the voices kept on coming regardless, compelling me to come to sufficiently at least to try and survey my surroundings.

I smacked my lips in an attempt to overcome the dryness of my mouth, at the same time putting my sunglasses back where they belonged—on my nose instead of resting on my cheek. Lazily lifting my head, I expected to find myself enveloped by a frolicking crowd of mere mortals. Instead, I found myself surrounded by an abundance of perfectly toned, tanned and attractive bodies. Obviously, I'd died and gone to Greek god and goddess heaven, I deduced. I was more than happy to be there, focusing all my attention on not one but quite a few of the Adonises surrounding me.

Then I realised I hadn't died at all. Bugger! I'd simply woken up.

I bolted upright intending to tidy myself up a bit. It very quickly became apparent that either I'd awakened to find myself slap bang in the middle of some glamorous photo shoot—one that I would, no doubt, be airbrushed out of thanks to my somewhat slovenly display—or that upon my arrival I'd accidentally chosen a section of the beach solely reserved for the island's 'beautiful people'. But whichever of the two it was, I was convinced someone was going to come along any second now, tap me on the shoulder and tell me to move on to the area set aside for the 'uglies' taking me to new levels in the embarrassment stakes!

I looked about me and, much to my disappointment, I saw that the climbers had at last descended from their great heights. I watched them partaking in a raucous game of football over to the left. *At least they know their place!* Not that I had any intentions of joining Team Ugly. After all, I might've been a little curvier than all these other women, but my curves were in all the right places. *Oh yes. I can carry a bikini off as well as the best of them. So just let anyone try and say different.*

I thought about all the time and money I'd spent over the years turning myself into the ideal woman for when I did happen to chance upon the man of my dreams: beauty products, waxing, exercising and dieting—the latter not exactly an easy task for a woman who loves her food. 'And let's not forget the elocution lessons,' I reminded myself, something which I doubted any of these ladies would deign to put themselves through. 'And surely it's time those efforts were rewarded somehow…' *Even if the prize is only to stake my claim on a bleedin' sunbed!* Although I knew I stood a better chance of not being booted off it if I actually looked the part, which needless to say called for a cool, calm and collected composure.

I began the process of arranging myself into a modelesque pose, a position that felt a lot more precarious than they'd made it out to be on those modelling TV shows. However, if I could just perfect my balance I was sure I'd be okay.

'Ouch!' I screamed as a searing sting suddenly swiped my face. Something ricocheted off it, catapulting me, legs akimbo, off my much-coveted sun lounger. 'What the...?' I shrieked, flying through the air, only to land in an undignified heap.

Cradling my face, I hastily scrambled back up onto my feet, desperately hoping against hope that none of my fellow beach users had actually witnessed this fall from grace. By virtue of the numerous sniggers sounding around me, however, it was clear my decorum had gone once and for all—no doubt because it had become attached to the offending football I could now see bouncing off into the distance.

'Jesus Christ! I'm so sorry!' a male voice called out.

I closed my eyes for a second, praying the culprit was one of the Greek gods, a deity now hell-bent on making it up to me. But as I looked up from dusting myself down, my heart sank. 'I might've known,' I cursed, instead seeing one of the scruffy climbers running towards me. Then again, with no dignity of their own to speak of I supposed it hardly surprising they couldn't consider anyone else's.

'Are you okay?' he asked.

Humiliation turned to annoyance. 'No thanks to you!' I replied.

'Let me see!' Without notice, the climber took hold of my face and tilted my head to one side.

'What're you doing?' I squealed, trying to wriggle free. But his grip was too firm and I was forced to wait it out. Being this up close and personal though, I recognised him: it was the guy from the boat, still wearing the same clothes, I noted. Although how often he did or didn't change his attire was hardly any of my business, no matter how gentle his touch turned out to be.

'There won't be any lasting damage,' he said, his middle-class inflection coming as a surprise taking into account his shabbiness, 'although it does look a bit red.'

At last he let go.

'I've told you,' I said, taking a step back. 'I'm fine.'

'At least let me buy you a drink or something,' he said, indicating the beach bar. 'By way of a proper apology.' He took a step forward, much to my irritation closing the gap between us once again. 'Look, I honestly didn't mean for that to happen.'

'I should hope not!' I said. 'Although I've a good mind to take you up on your offer and order the most expensive cocktail on the menu just out of spite.'

I couldn't really be that vindictive and, despite his sounding more posh than pauper, taking money from a penniless climber just wasn't my style. Plus, there was the fact that if I were to accept his offer, the outside world might think I was actually socialising with the man, something I most certainly had no intentions of doing. 'However, on this occasion I think I'll pass,' I said. 'You're just lucky I have everything I need here.' I indicated to my belongings, now strewn all over the place.

'Well, as long as you're sure,' he said rather sheepishly. 'That you're okay, I mean.'

His eyes looked directly into mine and I found myself coming over all strange. Probably concussion or something, I told myself. Or maybe even sunstroke—I had been asleep for some time.

'Sam!' one of his friends called out, evidently impatient for him to retrieve the ball so their game of footie could continue. 'In your own time, mate!'

He broke his gaze and signalled to his friend that he was coming.

'I'll leave you to it then,' he said.

'Yes,' I replied. 'I think you should.'

CHAPTER FOUR

Once for the thief, twice for the thief, three and it's his bad day.

S tanding there in my girly finery, groomed to perfection and my hair straightened to within an inch of its life, I looked out of place. As if the men weren't bad enough, it appeared even some of the female climbers didn't know how to run a brush through their hair and the place heaved with bodies, leaving me undecided as to whether to actually go in or not.

On the one hand, I thought everyone would be so engrossed in their own conversations they probably wouldn't even notice a woman spending an evening on her own with nothing but a book for company—something I definitely wasn't used to doing. On the other hand, by the very virtue of my singularity, I was convinced I'd stick out like a sore thumb.

'Lydia!' Efthimeos sang out, as if appearing from nowhere.
Shit!

'Please,' he encouraged. 'Come in. Sit.'

Now I didn't have a choice.

Despite my continued uncertainty, I followed in his footsteps, squeezing past one set of customers after another, in an attempt to get to the one and only vacant table. *Just my blooming luck.* I registered the noose hanging directly above it. *Although hardly surprising, considering the day I've had already.*

Against my better judgement, I took a seat.

'What would you like?' asked Efthimeos. 'Ouzo?' A cheeky smile spread across his face. 'Or maybe a Mythos?' he teased. 'I know how much you English like your beer.'

'Oh no,' I replied, shocked by the mere suggestion. It was one thing having to sit on my lonesome but quite another to be drinking on my own as well. 'Just a Coke for me, thank you.'

My host shook his head with what sounded like a heavy-hearted sigh. 'I understand,' he said. 'But how will you make friends if you don't relax?' He placed a comforting hand on my pitiful shoulder as he took himself off to get my equally pitiful drink, leaving me feeling somewhat awkward as I glanced around at my surroundings, just like the pitiful individual he clearly thought I was.

Nevertheless, everyone else was enjoying themselves; conversations about the day's events on the mountainside were coming at me from all directions.

'So how did you fair today?' I heard the young guy next to me ask his companions.

'Eight A ...' boasted the first, his smugness more than evident. 'On sight.'

'Seven A plus,' said the next, confident but not quite as self-righteous.

The third man fidgeted. 'Five B,' he said, barely audible—although what was wrong with that I was damned if I knew.

I supposed I could always ask, but even then, I doubted I'd understand. To me, their discussion sounded more like a dental check-up or grades on a school report card; in fact, they may as well have been speaking Greek.

I turned my attention to the bar area, smiling when I spotted the gorgeous Yiannis. He looked the complete pro as he got everyone's drinks orders together, expertly pouring one lethal-looking liquid after another into the various glasses sitting neatly in a line. *He certainly is handsome.* Then again, I wasn't his only admirer, I realised. The bevy of pretty yet muscular young things gathered around him obviously thought so too, causing me to take a deep breath and exhale, my shoulders visibly dropping in the process. *If only I was a few years younger!*

An excited squeal from Katerina snapped me back into the here and now and I turned, just in time to see her hold up a picture of a wedding gown featured in just one of the many wedding magazines she had piled in front of her. Her mum smiled at the image, before holding up one of her own and, although I couldn't understand the actual semantics of what they were both saying, I could tell by their gestures that they were comparing and contrasting, each eager to point out why one was better than the other.

I knew I shouldn't have come in. Pangs of jealousy suggested it should have been me and my mother having that conversation. But just because it wasn't, I supposed that didn't give me the right to begrudge the two of them their happiness, however much it felt like salt being rubbed into the wound. *You'll just have to find someone else's conversation to listen in on,* I told myself. *One that doesn't involve weddings or climbing.*

'Yiannis!' a male voice suddenly called out, followed by yet more incomprehensible Greek syllables.

'My friend! How are you?' lovely Yiannis replied.

Thankfully, this was a sentence I could understand and I assumed the newcomer must be something of a bi-lingual Englishman. *Very impressive.* I was keen to see who this disembodied voice belonged to.

'Sugar!' I said, immediately regretting my enthusiasm once I realised who the owner of the voice actually was. *What's he doing here?*

Following the incident at the beach, I had been hoping to avoid any future contact with Sam the Climber, yet here he was, larger than life. Not that I was sure which had bothered me the most—the football in the face, or the slightly unnerving eye contact. Neither of which I wanted to experience ever again and I wondered if I should just get up and leave while the going was good. But my drink still hadn't arrived and the last thing I wanted to do was look rude in of front Efthimeos. I had to think of something else and quick.

Grabbing my book from my bag, I opened it up and used it to shield my face. *This should do it!* However, just to make sure I began sinking lower and lower into my seat, until I was horizontal to the point I was almost on the floor. *Now he'll never notice me.*

I wondered if I should take a peek just to check on his whereabouts. But before I got the chance, a drink landing on the table in front of me caught my eye instead. It wasn't the simple glass of Coke I'd originally ordered, I further noticed, but some fancy fandangle cocktail.

I stared at the umbrellas, the tinsel and the cherries on sticks, not even daring to look up.

Please let it be Efthimeos… Please let it be Efthimeos… I plucked up the courage to lift my gaze. Unless my host had undergone some sort of superfast extreme makeover in the last few minutes, the game was up.

'There you go,' said Sam, indicating to the heavily adorned concoction. 'Not just my apology, but as requested, the most expensive drink on the menu.'

I put my book down and began the difficult task of hauling myself up into a more vertical position. 'I didn't request it,' I replied ungratefully. 'In fact, if I remember rightly, I said such a purchase wasn't necessary.'

My unwanted guest just carried on standing there, for some reason refusing to see this as his cue to leave—choosing instead to raise an eyebrow. He nodded to the drink. 'Aren't you going to at least try it?'

I considered his request for a moment, deciding it was a small price to pay if it meant getting rid of the man. And, duly picking up the glass and locating the straw from among all the flora and fauna, I took a long hard draw. 'Jesus, Mary and Joseph!' I spluttered, all at once choking and coughing. 'What the hell's in it? Meths?'

Sam laughed. 'A bit of everything,' he said. He plonked his beer down on the table and took a seat, uninvited.

'Excuse me if I don't share your amusement,' I replied, realising that was the second time that day he'd tried to kill me. 'And I don't remember asking you to join me either.'

There was something of a twinkle in his eye and, owing to his air of confidence, I could see that he was one of those men used to getting his own way when it came to members of the opposite sex. However, I'd met his type before and knew there was no way he'd ever come across the likes of me. Such a sparkle might've been enough to make any other girl go weak at the knees, but unlike theirs, my kneecaps were made of sterner stuff.

I picked up my book and tried to read, hoping he'd finally get the message that his presence wasn't wanted. But it was no good; he just sat there, seemingly as resolute in his desire to stay as I was determined he should leave. I could feel his eyes boring into me and, try as I might, I couldn't absorb a single word I read. *Why can't you just go back to your own kind?* I silently asked. *Instead of sitting here bothering me? And what do you want anyway?* Although I hazarded a pretty good guess.

I shifted in my seat, once again attempting to focus.

'You're not very friendly, are you?' he asked.

Admitting defeat, I snapped my book shut and dumped it on the table. 'And how friendly would you suggest I be with a man who uses my face for target practice?' I asked.

He let out a laugh, apparently viewing my question as more of an ice breaker than one that required an answer. 'I'm Sam,' he said, holding his hand out by way of a proper introduction.

'I heard,' I replied. 'Today at the beach.'

His arm remained outstretched, leaving me no choice but to concede. 'Lydia,' I said, accepting the handshake. 'Lydia Livingston.'

I watched him settle himself into a more comfortable position. *Great!* I thought. *Now he really is here for the long haul.*

'So, what brings you to these shores then, Lydia Livingston?'

'Not climbing, that's for sure.' I hoped the lack of a common interest would induce him to move on. Wishful thinking.

'I'd already gathered that,' he said, taking in my attire. At least I hoped it was my attire he was looking at.

I pulled my little cardi together just in case.

'Let me guess,' he continued, scrutinizing my face for clues.

This should be good, I thought. *Never in a million years is he gonna work out my backstory.*

'You're a high-flying company lawyer who just closed a billion-dollar deal. A holiday away from it all is your way of rewarding your achievement.'

I glared at him. 'Now you're just being sarcastic.'

'So, go on then, what is it you do? When you're not sunning yourself in the Hellenic Med, that is?'

I thought for a moment, wondering if I should just tell the truth—that I'd made a career out of searching for my lifelong companion and that I was in Kalymnos to come to terms with the fact that I'd failed. Of course, it was hardly my fault there didn't seem to be a man on the planet able to meet the requirements of the soulmate job spec, but I knew that wouldn't stop him from thinking I was barmy. And let's face it, if my own family didn't understand then I very much doubted a complete stranger would. Although the look on his face would be priceless, I realised, and a girl had to get her kicks from somewhere. Plus, telling him the truth would most certainly get rid of him; after all, when it came to men and this degree of honesty, it usually did.

'I'm a chef, if you must know,' I said, suddenly deciding to hell with the lot of it. I'd come here for a fresh start and the days of explaining myself were over. So, if that meant telling a little white lie in the interim so be it. Besides, it wasn't too much of a stretch considering my actual work place—or more to the point, if you discounted the fact that I couldn't cook. However, even that hadn't been for want of trying.

I thought back to the cookery classes I'd previously enrolled on, remembering how I'd expected to excel. As far as I was concerned, food preparation was the same as driving, in that any Tom, Dick or Harry could do it. Except, as it turned out, I was wrong. Not everyone had the necessary aptitude to follow a recipe, although, putting a positive slant on things, I didn't just fail the course.

According to the tutor I failed it spectacularly—which in my view had to be better than failing miserably.

'In fact, I have my own restaurant,' I continued—simply because I could. 'A very successful restaurant I might add, if I do say so myself.'

Sam let out a whistle. 'I'm impressed. A woman with beauty and who knows the way straight to a man's heart.'

I smiled. *Maybe I was right earlier?* Maybe I should be an actress? The man obviously believes every word I'm saying, so I must have some talent.

'Yes, I'm here for research purposes,' I said, by now really getting into character. 'To sample traditional Greek food at its finest, so to speak.'

'Yiannis!' Sam suddenly called out, following this with an indecipherable string of verbals—verbals that to a mono-lingual like me made absolutely no sense at all.

And just when I was on a roll, too.

Nevertheless, and whatever the translation, as I looked over to the Fatolitis family, it appeared Yiannis felt excited enough to impart what he'd just heard to his father, who then animatedly passed on the information to his wife and daughter; only for the two of them to start nudging each other and looking my way as well, all the while demonstrating their delight over what they now knew.

'What?' I asked, slight nerves setting in. 'What did you say?'

'Just that we have a famous chef in the house,' said Sam, all innocence and smiles. 'Why? Was it meant to be a secret?'

I looked back to my host family, momentarily optimistic that Sam hadn't told them anything of the sort; that he was lying to me, in the same way I'd just lied to him. But with the Fatolitis clan continuing to somewhat colourfully gesticulate my way, I had no choice but to acknowledge he was, indeed, telling me the truth.

In that instant, not only could I have kicked myself for opening my own big mouth, I could've kicked Sam for not keeping his shut. The last thing I'd wanted was for my exaggerations to be broadcast—to them of all people. As far as I was concerned, the Fatolitis felt sorry for me enough already because of my single status, so goodness knew what their reaction would be if they ever found out I'd invented a whole new life for myself to boot.

I decided the situation called for a bit of damage limitation. 'I hardly said I was famous,' I replied. 'I mean, just because a girl cooks for a living.'

'Oh, I don't know,' said Sam, refusing to follow my lead. 'I bet if I was to go over to that computer and put your name in Google, as a bona fide restaurateur, your name would be on there somewhere.'

I followed his gaze, doing my utmost to maintain at least some level of composure. *Shit!* I almost freaked at the sight of a computer. Up until then, I hadn't even noticed the sodding thing sitting in the far corner; the one with the FREE WI-FI sign emblazoned on the wall next to it. How could I have been so stupid? And why hadn't I realised he'd think to do something like that in the first place? Especially when hitting the net was exactly what I, myself, would've done were there even a whiff of anyone potentially interesting in the vicinity.

'I shouldn't think so,' I said, desperately trying to think on my feet. 'We don't advertise, you see. We don't need to. We get all our custom through word of mouth.'

'That good, eh?' said Sam, appearing genuinely interested. 'Although you'd be surprised. Everyone's on there somewhere.' He rose to his feet. 'Come on, I'll show you.'

'You're joking, aren't you?' I asked, hopeful.

'No, not at all,' he said. 'Why?'

'Because it'll be embarrassing,' I replied—although admittedly, not quite in the way he was obviously thinking.

'Don't be daft. You should be proud of your achievements. And besides, it'll be fun.'

Oh God, and with things very quickly going from bad to worse, the situation called for a much-needed drink.

I picked up the initially unwanted cocktail accordingly, had a bit of a fight with the glitzy foliage and, finally able to locate the straw from within, took a very long slurp.

'You go ahead,' I said, feeling my fake professional poise beginning to slip somewhat. 'I'll just finish this and then I'll be over to join you.'

'No worries,' said Sam. 'Although you'll have to give me the name.'

'Sorry?' I replied, momentarily confused.

'The name? Of your establishment?'

I anxiously looked about myself, hastily trying to come up with a suitable restaurant moniker, my eyes finally settling on my book. 'Austen's,' I said, inwardly flinching at the sheer desperation of it all. 'Yes, Austen's.'

Much to my relief, Sam didn't pick up on my angst. In fact, as I watched him head off, he was more than happy to be making his way through the throng of customers and over to that damn machine. I wondered just how long his contentment would last once he realised I'd told him a pack of lies—not that I planned on sticking around long enough to actually find out.

With nothing else for it, I dispensed with the straw and drinks foliage altogether and in one long glug downed the rest of my drink. Then, as I waited for him to settle himself down in front of the monitor, all the while desperate to get out of there, I took a quick gander about me to make sure no one was watching, gathered up my belongings and stole off into the night.

CHAPTER FIVE

The kettle rolled down and found the lid.

W*hat were you thinking?* I was stuck in the middle of the madness that was Pothia. This was my first visit back since landing on the boat from Kos.

The sun battered down, I was sweltering beyond belief, and my head pounded from the noise of the incessant traffic. A never-ending trail of vehicles zoomed by at breakneck speed in one circular motion on the one circular road that looped its way in and out of the town.

A sudden beeping sounded from behind and I spun around to spot a scooter heading directly towards me. 'Jesus Christ!' I screamed, quickly leaping out of its path. However, the offending two-wheeler careered straight past without even the slightest of hesitations, leaving me not just gobsmacked at the rider's complete lack of consideration, but also questioning who was actually in more danger here, me or his side-saddling elderly female passenger?

Road safety concerns were seriously lacking here and the whole place felt like an accident waiting to happen. And how on earth does a motorised two-wheeler manage to stay upright when it's carrying a family of four, their pet dog and the kitchen sink anyway? Moreover, I couldn't count on one hand the number of fast moving cars with their front ends missing that I encountered, let alone the fare-shifting trucks on their road to nowhere. In fact, all this commotion made me wonder how much more my stress levels could physically take, such was the urban restlessness going on around me.

Then again, there wasn't much common courtesy taking place among the pedestrians when it came to their manoeuvrings either, I noted, as I was forced to dodge my way around yet another passer-by—an action that felt just as dangerous as avoiding the horrendous traffic and, with jeopardy coming at me from all angles, it really did feel like I was taking part in some sort of extreme hazard perception test.

Still, unlike back in Massouri, at least down here you're not going to be singled out. I was desperately trying to remain positive. I ignored the little whispers suggesting anyone and everyone, be they in vehicles or on foot, were indeed trying to pick me off.

Who on earth tries to pass themselves off as a renowned chef, for goodness sake, and thinks they can actually get away with it? I deemed it nothing short of a miracle that I'd so far managed to avoid the fact that I was by now, no doubt, the complete laughing stock of the place. Although at the same time I did have to admit this had taken a lot of ducking and diving on my part, sneaking about here, there and everywhere so I wouldn't be seen.

Hence this rather fraught visit to Pothia.

In my view, there were only so many times a woman could endure the long haul up and over the hill to the other side of Massouri because the walk straight through the village felt too much of a risk. And despite the trek being a diversion more than worth the exertion, especially if it meant I could continue to save face, my legs still felt in urgent need of a break.

As if you don't need the exercise though, I thought, catching sight of my reflection in a shop window. *So just think of all the calories you've been burning.*

Not that my legs were getting their well-earned respite from all that hiking anyway, I realised, what with all the shops and stores raised up from the road to lofty heights as they were. Regrettably, for shorties like me, this meant there weren't any pavements as such, just one long, narrow platform to negotiate, broken up every now and then by an inconveniently placed junction. A flood defence as opposed to a real sidewalk, of course;

although understandably so considering everything was built into the mountainside. But, at knee level, it was becoming a bit of a pain having to keep hoisting myself first up and then down the damn thing, just to be able to browse the various wares on offer. And of course, between all that hoisting and stretching, due to being only five foot two, there was still the fear-inducing traffic and Kamikaze pedestrians to consider. Suffice to say, the look wasn't good.

I sighed, fed up with making a show of myself.

As well as cheering myself up with a bit of spending, it had been my intention to pick up a few gifts to take back to England with me, but so far I'd failed to come up trumps on both counts. *Surely there has to be a souvenir shop somewhere?* I had thought it obligatory for a holiday destination to purvey a range of fridge magnets, local trinkets and naff T-shirts.

However, everything here looked to be geared towards the needs of the island's local people and their everyday lives rather than towards the likes of me. *Which I suppose is fair enough,* I conceded, even if it wasn't very helpful.

Oh, I don't know. Maybe I should just give up on the whole shopping thing. I took another glance up and down the street.

That was when I saw it.

With a quick look left and right, I raced over to the other side of the street, this time more than happy to car dodge and heave myself up onto the unforgiving platform in yet another unbecoming clamber. And, pressing my hands and face against the glass of the one shop guaranteed to satisfy my need for retail therapy, I couldn't quite believe a store trading solely in sunglasses even existed. I almost drooled like some starving waif on the wrong side of a restaurant window, marvelling at the display before me. 'Oh my goodness,' I said, eagerly scanning the shop's contents. Gucci, Police, Prada, Ray Ban… they were all there and none of them that fake rubbish you could pick up at the market for a fiver either. Oh no, these were the real McCoy, I excitedly noted, and all together in one exhibit, all calling out to me in unison.

Lydia…! Lydia…! Lydia…! They chanted, doing their utmost to lure me inside.

I tried to ignore the temptation. After all, didn't I have enough designer sets to my name already? But that didn't stop me wanting to go inside. *I suppose I could get Mum a pair?* This gave me just the excuse I needed. *I think she'd look quite the femme fatale in a nice pair of Dolce and Gabbanas.* But, just as I was about to reach for the handle to open the shop door, I hesitated, feeling that initial buzz of excitement start to wane.

Even if I did fork out that kind of cash on her behalf, at those prices I knew she'd probably be too scared to wear them anyway. She wouldn't be able to enjoy them in the same way I would for fear of losing them and even if a practical rather than fashionable woman like my mother was able to overcome such concerns, they'd still only remain in their box untouched thanks to the good old English weather, which isn't exactly renowned for its hours and hours of glorious sunshine. And, considering Mum and Dad hadn't ever left their home country, it wasn't as if Mum could save them for her summer holidays, now was it? In fact, the more I thought about it, the more I wasn't particularly sure if *either* of my parents even possessed a passport.

Disappointed, I peeled myself away from the window, forced to rethink my ideas.

Which reminds me, I still haven't rung home.

Deep down, I knew the lack of communication hadn't been a complete slip of the mind; I had been putting it off somewhat. Although as far as I was concerned with good reason, considering I didn't have a clue how to respond when the inevitable questions arose, when they enquired as to what I'd been up to during my stay and how it was all going.

I suppose I could always make something up? Tell them it's all going swimmingly?

But then again, wasn't being less than truthful the very thing that got you into this mess in the first place?

Not only that, I acknowledged. Mum has always had a knack of seeing straight through me whenever I've had cause to be less than honest. And as she's also the one who nine times out of ten answers the telephone, telling another little white lie isn't really an option, however attractive it might seem.

I could just imagine the conversation.

'So, come on then,' Mum would say. 'What's it like out there? How are you getting on?'

'Oh, everything's fine,' I'd have to reply. 'Apart from the fact that I accidentally told a big, fat fib, that is. One that everybody now knows about. So, having banished myself from England to reconsider my uncertain future, I now have to deal with the serious possibility of deporting myself from Kalymnos as well. But other than that, I'd say it's all going pretty well really... Anyway, what about you lot? How are things at home?'

Of course, they wouldn't be surprised to hear I'd made a bit of hash of things out here in Greece. All the other Livingstons thought me as daft as a brush to begin with, but still, that didn't make getting in touch with them any easier. The last thing I wanted to hear right now was 'I told you so', a phrase they'd undoubtedly use, especially when they hadn't wanted me to leave England from the start. With my birthday fast looming they'd wanted me to stay at home and celebrate in the same way we always did—with an extra family get-together. These events were very much like our ritual Sunday lunch gatherings, only on birthdays we got jelly and ice cream, candles, and a cake.

My birthday. I didn't really want to think about it.

Despite all the bus windows being open, the air felt oppressive and positively second hand, which I supposed wasn't any wonder considering the vast number of people shoehorned into the vehicle. Still, I might've been seriously hot and bothered but at least I had a seat, even if the old chap squeezed in next to me did wear a toothless smile and looked about a hundred and ten years old.

Unlike the poor buggers crammed into the aisles. Although to be fair, the standing-room-only crowd did appear to consist of mainly climbers whose limbs could take the strain. All of them were taking a breather from their mountainside pursuits if the snippets of conversation I heard were anything to go by, and all apparently unfazed by their lack of personal space.

I glanced about at the other passengers: mainly Greek women with numerous children and grandchildren between them. And something of a lively crowd; they all shouted across to each other through the throng, nattering nineteen to the dozen and speaking with their hands as much as they were with their tongues. In fact, the only time any of them quietened was when they paid their respects to the dead, an action that involved making numerous signs of the cross, one after the other, every time we passed some church or religious monument.

I could tell by their excitable tone that they were exchanging the latest in gossip, and it wouldn't have surprised me if this included a conversation about the mad English woman.

'Have you heard about the basket case who's tried to pass herself off as a chef?' one of them was probably asking.

'Not just any old chef,' another would be laughing. 'But a famous one at that!'

I recoiled at the shame of it all.

With nothing else for it, I decided to zone out of the tittle-tattle altogether and turn my attention to what was going on outside the bus. I recognised some of the landmarks I'd seen during the taxi ride upon my initial arrival and, once again, I couldn't fail to be impressed as the *Wow!* view appeared on the horizon. However, as we began to follow the winding road that led straight down into Massouri, I could feel my body start to tense and with my heart rate beginning to pick up pace, I had to steel myself in readiness for being spotted. The finger pointing and sniggering was something I most definitely wasn't looking forward to. It was all my own doing, I knew that, but it didn't make the prospect of facing up to my misdemeanour any easier. Being the laughing stock just wasn't my style.

Suddenly, the bus took a right turn and began meandering up and over the hill, the very same one that bypassed the village altogether. *Thank God.* I was finally able to exhale, and as my shoulders slumped with relief, it seemed I'd got away with it for another day. Phew! I could relax.

Continuing to stare out of the window, I realised that despite having made my way along this road on a number of occasions before, I'd never taken the time to actually absorb the scenery. Previously, I'd been more concerned with catching my breath during the hike up as opposed to enjoying what was around me, up until now remaining completely oblivious to the whole new, more far-reaching vista.

From here it wasn't just Talendos I could see, and I dug out my tourist map to identify exactly which other places I was now looking at. There was the next neighbouring island of Leros, then out into the distance was Patmos and, squinting a little, I was convinced even Ikaria was on display. And the romantic in me readily pretended the big yacht in the midst of all these was really the giant sailing boat, the *Argo*, making its way over to Asia Minor in search of the Golden Fleece.

All of it was a world away from the civilization inland, mostly in the form of houses dotted along the roadside. Some of them were more like mountainside mansions than mere residencies or villas, even if the pillars and fancy ironwork were a bit gaudy for my taste. But considering the views on offer, it was hardly surprising the wealthy of the island would choose a spot like this to build a house. *Yep, there's some serious money up here.* The bus passed a garden fountain. It was a giant stone carp with water gushing from its mouth. *It's just a shame they don't all have the class to go with it.*

A female passenger got up from her seat and pressed one of the vehicle's stop buttons, signalling it was time for her to get off. Not that she appeared particularly well-to-do, I noted, but I supposed appearances could be deceiving. *Either that or she's one of the inhabitants' servants,* I considered. *I mean, with this kind of cash it's not as if they'd do their own cleaning around here, is it?*

The bus came to a slow standstill, giving me the chance to have a nosey into the grounds of one of the properties. *How the other half lives, eh?* I thought, watching some chap next to the biggest barbecue I'd seen in my life. *You could get a fair amount of chicken legs on that!*

I focused my attention and became momentarily confused. *Hang on a minute… It can't be.*

But, unquestionably, as I scrutinized the man some more it was definitely Sam the Climber I was espying, of all people. *And looking very much at home!*

He was either preparing or cleaning the barbecue, I struggled to tell which. Although as I slunk down in my seat, determined he wouldn't see me in return, I wondered what he'd be doing in a big house like that in the first place. After all, running the air conditioning alone would cost an absolute fortune, never mind the monthly rent. *Very strange.* I thought a run-down shack would be more his style.

He seemed something of a fixture and fitting around these parts. Not only did he speak the language, if his relationship with the Fatolitis was anything to go by, people certainly trusted him. So, it stood to reason he'd be doing odd jobs for the locals during his stay, I surmised, as his way of earning a bit of cash while he's here.

The bus began to set off again and we left Sam behind.

Not that it's got anything to do with you anyway. I remembered the immediacy of my own problems. *You've enough to think about when it comes to your own time on the island, never mind anybody else's!*

CHAPTER SIX

If you join the dance circle you must dance.

I dragged my feet as I made my way back after yet another day at the beach; after all, there's only so much time an individual can spend on their own without it having some sort of ill effect. And while my tan might've been coming along nicely thank you very much, this living in isolation business didn't half feel boring—especially for a social butterfly like me. In fact, even the Livingston chaos was preferable to this insularity, to the point that as I snuck up the steps that led up the side of the Fatolitis to my apartment, I thought I must be going a bit mad. Let's face it—why else would I be craving Pete's constant jibes or the twins' incessant noise? And why else would I have started talking out loud to myself?

However, as I rummaged for my key, I also knew this predicament was all of my own doing and that I had to just grin and bear the lack of company—unless I was prepared to admit the truth, that was, which I most certainly wasn't.

A plastic container on the patio table suddenly caught my eye, bringing a welcome diversion for my thoughts. Curious, as it hadn't been there earlier and realising that while I'd been out I must have had a visitor, I didn't know whether to feel disappointed at not having been around to greet them, or, because of my circumstances, relieved for the exact same reason.

Well, whoever it was they came bearing gifts. I picked up the accompanying handwritten note. But much to my bemusement it contained only a single word with absolutely nothing to indicate who it was from. 'Enjoy', it simply said, although not in the neatest of scripts.

Lifting the container, I could see it was some kind of food and the box felt warm too, so whoever had come I must've only just missed them. Moreover, as I opened the lid, careful not to spill the contents, I found the most delicious looking meal I'd had the pleasure of seeing in days staring straight back at me ... big chunks of beef and juicy shallots in the most mouth-watering of tomato sauces, and all just at that ready-to-eat temperature. The one at which food undoubtedly tastes its best.

'*Stifado...*' I sighed.

Remembering it from one of the restaurant menus, I breathed in its superb aroma, unsure whether to laugh or cry. Laugh in a hallelujah kind of way because I was starving; or cry because someone could be having a joke at my expense, on account of me claiming I was something of a chef myself. *Not that you're going to eat any of it.* I was determined to ignore the fact that I hadn't had a decent meal in days, no matter how appealing it looked. 'The way things are that would be just plain wrong.'

On the other hand, for a food loving non-cook like myself, I didn't know how much longer I could survive without a decent meal inside me, especially as for the past few days I'd been living on the provisions purchased upon my arrival. Yoghurt and honey... bread and cheese... ham and salad... basically all the stuff that didn't involve any particular skill when it came to preparation and all bought at a time when I could unashamedly wander to the local shop in the village square without condemnation.

However, while it had been possible to find a quiet, secluded spot on the beach from which I could stave off prying eyes and pointing fingers, it wasn't as if there'd be any such privacy in a crowded eating establishment. *Which is a shame considering all the great restaurants in the area. Greek, French, Italian... all nationalities catered for.*

I bemoaned the fact that I wasn't able to visit any of them now, owing to my self-imposed hermit-like existence, and, even though this unexpected gift was just what both my belly and I needed, taking everything into account, I knew I couldn't eat it. *Life can be so cruel sometimes…*

'Although it does look very tempting.' I wavered, telling myself the meal could've come from the Fatolitis, their pity now at its highest. In their view, not only was I forced to holiday on my own as a result of my being a pathetic Billy No Mates, but I'd since seen fit to embellish on my life as well, which could only translate as me not having a life, full stop. Which meant as far as they were concerned it was no wonder I was forced to hole myself up indoors twenty-four-seven, all the while wasting away to a mere skeleton. Starving to death, such was my shame, because I clearly couldn't face the ridicule of being seen out in public. And apart from the fact that I had managed to sneak out into the fresh air every day, I did have to admit they'd be right.

Or maybe it's from Sam. This could be his way of letting me know he's on to me? His way of having the last laugh?

My mind began to really run away with itself, conspiracy theories abounding.

Worse still, the Fatolitis could be in on the whole thing with him. And it's a case of them all having a good giggle at my expense…

I cringed. Surely even I didn't deserve that? Or did I?

I wondered how they could do this to me. I took the plastic box inside and flung it down onto the kitchen counter. 'Well, you're not going to get away with it,' I declared, determined to show everyone I wasn't the fool they obviously took me for. 'Oh no… nobody laughs at Lydia Livingston and gets away with it!'

I should've just tossed the container straight in the bin, then it wouldn't matter how many times its contents called out to me—I still wouldn't be able to eat them. But the meal smelled way too wonderfully fantastic to throw out. With a bit of luck, the aroma alone would be enough to satisfy my need for something good and meaty to eat.

Wafting the air around the box my way, I continued to tell myself just the bouquet would suffice. However, with my mouth salivating and my belly grumbling, I realised this probably wasn't going to be the case. *Bugger it!* I swiftly grabbed a spoon from the cutlery drawer, having decided just one mouthful alone couldn't do any harm, now could it?

'Mmmm.' I chewed, savouring the taste… all the while lost in gourmet heaven.

Of course, I couldn't have fathomed that one spoonful would quickly turn into two, then three and then four… and that before I knew it, I'd be spooning out the tomato-based remnants stuck to the bottom of the now noticeably empty Tupperware.

That's done it.

I rubbed my satisfied stomach, thinking that a nice glass of wine would be just the thing to wash such gorgeous food down with. The trouble was, with my stomach now fit to burst, I realised there was no way I could manage the trek up and over the hill for a sneak visit to the shop. At least, not unless I was happy to vomit the whole meal back up again on the way.

Although I could always nip downstairs. They do have wine down there.

But even so, I still wasn't sure coming face to face with the Fatolitis was really a good idea.

I stared at the empty container, telling myself I was going to have to look them in the eye at some stage. 'Especially now you might just have troughed their food…'

'And just because you don't have honesty on your side at the moment,' I continued, 'that doesn't mean you don't have manners.' Something Mum had instilled in all her children since the day we could talk.

Steeling myself, ready to do the inevitable, it felt like one of those now or never moments—one where I knew I simply had to take the bull by the horns come what may and just get on with it. *Yes, this mess has gone on far too long as it is. So, come on, Lydia, it's time to face up to things.*

I grabbed my bag and headed for the door before I could change my mind. But as I let myself out of the apartment and made my way back down the steps, any conviction I'd been feeling quickly turned into a sense of trepidation. The last thing I wanted was for people to start giggling and talking about me behind their hands as if to say, 'Here she is, the wannabe chef.' However, as I turned the corner, it seemed the gods were actually on my side for a change.

'Thank you, Lord,' I said, pleased that there didn't appear to be many customers on the premises at all.

This more relaxed environment should've made going in that little bit easier, but I still felt nervous—especially when there was a good chance I could be chased straight back out again at any given moment. And, although it may be quiet now, the Greeks had proven themselves to be quite a passionate lot during my stay, sounding like they were arguing even when they weren't. *So goodness knows what they sound like when they really do have a gripe.*

I caught sight of Efthimeos, deep in thought and, talk about a negative omen, playing with a string of worry beads of all things.

'Lydia,' he called out, suddenly jumping to attention upon spotting my arrival. He began animatedly gesturing to the rest of the family, Maria and Katerina now also springing to their feet to hail my arrival. Their actions were enough to make me think, fingers crossed, that my earlier fears just might have been unfounded.

'More wishful thinking,' I told myself, the cynical side of me automatically questioning their motives. As far as I was concerned, no one in their right mind could continue to be this welcoming when it came to someone in my position and I wondered if this treatment of me really was their way of welcoming the pitiable young woman back into the fold, or, regardless of any untruths, a tactic because they were glad of my custom.

Probably the latter, I thought uncharitably. *After all, business is business.*

Rather unnervingly, the three of them couldn't seem to do enough. Naturally, I wasn't going to complain; in my view, this over the top treatment was far better than the alternative. And besides, still on the business front—they couldn't exactly come out and call me a downright liar, could they? Not when I was renting their upstairs apartment—the customer is always right philosophy and all that jazz.

'Lydia, come…' said Katerina, both she and her mother hastily beckoning me forward.

'Please…' said Efthimeos, motioning me to a seat—this time steering me away from the dreaded noose, thank goodness.

'Where have you been,' continued Katerina. She produced a cloth and began expertly wiping down my perfectly clean table somewhat unnecessarily. Well, unnecessary if you disregarded her checking out her own reflection in the glass, that is. 'We've been worried about you.'

I watched Maria hurriedly head off before reappearing with a little bowl of peanuts to accompany my as yet unordered drink and despite her not being able to verbalize what she wanted to say owing to the language barrier. I found her kind, softly smiling eyes to be both welcoming and embracing. She obviously wasn't as good at playing the game as the rest of them, and I took this as a sign of her sympathy.

God, this is awful. I decided it might've been better to have them screaming and shouting at me, after all. In fact, completely ignoring me had to be better than this embarrassment.

In fact, it was Yiannis alone who didn't make any fuss as such; from his position behind the bar he simply proffered a wave, which was very much to my relief considering pity from a guy like him just wouldn't have done.

He gave his wave an accompanying smile and, despite being already seated, I still found myself coming over all weak at the knees. *Then again, to have someone like that fawning over me whatever the reason wouldn't really be a bad thing.* Although at the same time, I did have to admit his doing so because he found me irresistibly, drop-dead gorgeous would ultimately be so much better.

'What would you like?' asked Efthimeos, forcing me to leave all thoughts of you know what behind.

'Sorry? Oh… Just a glass of wine, please,' I replied, finally able to remember what it was I'd actually come in for.

'Red or white?' he asked.

'Erm, red if you've got it.'

He nodded to his son and in something of a whirlwind, Yiannis was on the job of pouring it, Katerina dutifully delivered it and, before I knew it, the father of the family was seemingly anticipating my opinion on it. Naturally, this sudden extra keenness to their behaviour felt more than a tad bemusing and as Efthimeos continued to expectantly hover, it felt like I had no choice but to play along.

I looked down at the glass in front of me with no idea as to what did or didn't constitute a good claret. At the same time, I was wondering how on earth, out of all the courses I'd taken, I could've missed signing up for wine tasting classes. However, looking back to Efthimeos, thanks to his eagerness the pressure was certainly on to at least pretend I knew what I was doing, no matter how silly I felt. I tentatively picked up the glass and took a bit of a sip accordingly.

I swished it around my mouth for a moment, something I'd seen the professionals do on television. Of course, that was when they went on to spit the liquid out, which I most certainly wasn't going to do. Instead, I took the only other option and swallowed, before pausing as if still contemplating its taste.

The whole family was on pins as they waited for me to deliver my verdict. Although why they cared quite so much was a bit of a conundrum to me.

'Very nice,' I eventually said.

The collective sigh of relief that followed was more than audible, but it appeared the Fatolitis still weren't ready to relax just yet.

'And the food?' asked a cautious Efthimeos. 'You enjoyed that too?'

My heart skipped a beat. So, the meal did come from the Fatolitis.

I looked from my host to the rest of the family, wondering if it had been some sort of elaborate trap to get me down here so they could challenge me on my lies. But they all appeared innocent enough.

I shifted in my seat. 'Food?'

'The *Stifado*,' Efthimeos clarified. 'Did you like it?'

His demeanour displayed a genuine concern, making it clear the dinner had been a compassionate offering as opposed to anything more sinister. Looking around, I told myself that *I* could pretend everything was normal and that I hadn't really said what I'd said that night if *they* could.

'Oh yes,' I replied. 'It was very nice, thank you.'

Efthimeos visibly relaxed.

'Hence, the glass of wine,' I pointed out. 'It would've been lovely to have with the meal, but seeing as I didn't have any...'

I watched him go from relieved to panic stricken in an instant. 'Lydia,' he said. 'You want wine in your room?'

Again, I looked from him to the others—all of them seemingly aghast at the mere suggestion. Why could I not keep my blooming mouth shut? Now they thought I was a raving alcoholic on top of everything else. Not that this should've come as any great surprise, I supposed, not after every other character flaw I'd shown myself to possess.

'You should have said,' Efthimeos continued.

The man's statement threw me. After all, one minute he's scolding me for having some sort of liquid dependency, yet in the next, he's actively encouraging it.

Speaking in forked tongue, he called out to his son and quick as anything, Yiannis was reaching for a bottle of wine and a clean wine glass and placing both of them on a tray—obviously in preparation for taking them up to my apartment.

'No, no,' I said, trying to dismiss all thoughts of Yiannis, me and a bottle of wine all in the same room together. 'That's not necessary. This is plenty.' I pointed to my glass. 'Thank you.'

Efthimeos appeared hurt and for some reason at pains to make sure I wanted for nothing.

'Honestly,' I said, doing my utmost to reassure him. 'I'm fine.'

'But the food?' he said. 'That was good?'

'Yes,' I replied and feeling like I was in some sort of twilight zone, I just wished we could all get back to the pretence. 'It was very good.'

'Maria is an excellent cook,' Efthimeos explained. 'She can give you the... the...' He struggled to come up with the right word.

'Recipe,' Yiannis called out.

'Yes, recipe,' Efthimeos repeated. 'Would you like it?'

As confusing as this question felt, I thought back to my cookery classes and as kind as the offer was, I doubted it would be of any use to me, a fact with which Efthimeos disagreed.

'It might help?' he suggested.

It was one thing he knew I wasn't the cordon bleu guru I'd claimed to be, but quite another to know just how lacking a chef I was in reality. Although how Sam the Climber had managed to uncover my kitchen mishaps on the net alongside my non-identity goodness only knew.

'It might help with your, er...' Efthimeos carried on.

'Research,' finished Yiannis.

My eyes widened in horror as realisation dawned.

Oh... my... God...! I thought, forced to swallow the accompanying yelp before it managed to escape my lips. None of this charade is out of pity. It's because they still think I'm some famous chef from England...!

What was it I'd said? *Oh yes... I'm here to sample Greek food at its finest.* I was forced to acknowledge with rhetoric like that it was no wonder the Fatolitis had taken me at my word. Cringing at the muddle I'd got myself into, I realised my greed had only gone and made things worse. Why hadn't I just thrown that damned container in the bin?

I felt the colour begin to drain from my face as I began to imagine myself unwittingly tucking into their hearty offering.

'Are you okay, Lydia?' asked Efthimeos, coming over all anxious.

'I'll get you some water,' said Katerina, making me feel even more of a fraud.

'I'm fine,' I replied, my voice suddenly taking on a squeak-like quality and as I looked to my hosts I was no longer sure how to respond to their kind hospitality. I could've kicked myself for my stupidity over everything I'd said and done during my stay. These people had been nothing but kind, and as it turns out had done everything in their power to help me in my so-called culinary quest, completely unaware that their support had been based on a falsehood.

You could always own up, I told myself. That would be the right thing to do.

However, as I looked from Efthimeos to the others and back again, I wasn't sure which would be worse: the suffering I'd up until now endured over the prospect of the Fatolitis knowing the absolute truth about me? Or having to live through the deception of it all if I did, indeed, keep up the lie?

CHAPTER SEVEN

For the nail, he lost the horseshoe.

'That was superb, Maria,' I said, such was the feast that she'd just bestowed upon us and although she probably didn't understand my words I kissed my fingers like any good food expert would, in a universal gesture that *everyone* could comprehend. I quite enjoyed the fact that the Fatolitis had taken to inviting me down to the bar to eat with them—during the late afternoon lull, the time just before the run of evening customers began descending on the place. Not only was it nice to be a part of a family again, what with mine thousands of miles away, Maria's cooking was sublime and I found myself rubbing my overly stuffed belly after the *Kleftiko* that had been on tonight's menu, a mixture of melt-in-the-mouth lamb, olive oil, oregano and garlic. Sheer bliss to the taste buds, as were all of this woman's creations, including her *Dolmades, Soutzoukakia* and *Spanakopita*, each of which I'd previously had the honour of sampling thanks to her hospitality.

'Bravo,' she replied, delighting in my response and, although, at first, I'd felt guilty about deceiving them all with my pork pie of a motive for stuffing my face on a daily basis, seeing the lady of the house's response every time I offered my feedback was actually quite priceless. To the point that it was almost as enjoyable as tasting her food itself—I'd begun to feel the initial untruth between us become less and less of an issue.

I wondered what it was about mothers and food. They loved to watch the rest of the family tucking into a nice, home-cooked dinner. My own mum was the same, of course. One word of praise and it made her entire day. However, any gratitude in the offering usually came from me, probably because out of all of us, I was the one who knew first-hand that cooking wasn't as easy as she managed to make it look. In fact, as far as the other Livingstons were concerned, I think eating was more of a necessity than a pleasure. There was no savouring but merely lots of swallowing, and when the food went down it probably didn't even touch the sides. No wonder my dad and brothers constantly suffered from indigestion.

And maybe it's the same for Maria, I thought, returning her sunbeam smile with one of my own. Maybe her cooking is just taken for granted too, even if this family did know how to chew.

We'd developed a sort of routine to these culinary events, a routine similar to the family gatherings that took place back home—one where the men simply partook in the actual eating of the meal while the women's role included either the food's preparation before consumption or the cleaning up afterwards. Needless to say, my extra responsibilities fell into the latter category. I didn't mind though. Under the circumstances I knew full well the washing up was the least I could do.

'I suppose I should get to it,' I said, heaving myself up onto my feet to gather everyone's plates up. Katerina followed me out to the kitchen to start preparing the after dinner coffees. I ran the taps, ready to immerse myself in the task at hand.

'So, you're looking forward to the big day then? You're not getting nervous?' I asked, adding a squirt of washing up liquid into the sink. 'About the wedding, I mean.'

Katerina stopped what she was doing. 'I can't wait,' she replied. 'Everything is booked and arranged. Also I have my gown… I have the flowers…' she sang. 'And I have my groom,' she added with a bit of a giggle; she was clearly besotted with the man.

'Not too long to wait now, eh?' I said, determined to keep my envy of the girl in check.

'Not long at all,' she replied, suddenly losing herself in the anticipation of it all. 'Oh, Lydia, I am so excited. And you should see my dress—it's so glamorous and fitted in all the right places.' She ran her hands down the sides of her body as if to emphasize her point. 'I will be like an angel,' she continued. 'A beautiful angel.'

Not so long ago I'd have thought her ramblings and confident self-image rather conceited; she did have a habit of coming across as loving herself a little too much. But because of these dinners I'd got to know her a bit more and my pangs of envy and fleeting annoyances were somewhat easier to cope with. Now I could see she wasn't just a young woman who happened to be considerably aware of her physical attributes, but a young woman about to do the one thing she'd spent her whole life planning, in very much the same way I had. In fact, Katerina was probably the only female I knew of who might understand exactly where I'd been coming from all these years. Here on this little island, dreams of getting married and being a homemaker—and a homemaker alone—were more than acceptable; unlike where I came from, where it was deemed politically incorrect to have such aspirations, what with it being the twenty-first century and all that.

I watched her get back to making the coffees, even managing to raise a smile as I realised we had things other than our hopes and dreams in common. We were both the baby in our families for one, although I could see she was more spoiled than I was. We also both had brothers for siblings, despite me having to put up with two of them when she was lucky enough to only have one. Although I couldn't quite imagine the lovely Yiannis ever trying to string Katerina to a tree so he could pelt her with water bombs like Pete and Steve had done with me. My lips curled into another smile. *Oh no, Yiannis was far too good-looking to behave in any way as nasty as that.*

The clattering of china as Katerina began setting cups on a tray brought my thoughts back to reality, her dream-like humming serving to remind me of the one very distinct difference between us—the fact that she'd managed to succeed in her marital ambitions, when I most certainly hadn't; I sighed. *Life can be cruel sometimes.* I silently acknowledged that my situation had nothing to do with the girl before me. *So why shouldn't she bask in the glory of her up-and-coming nuptials?*

Besides, what will be, will be, I supposed, resigned to my fate. For some of us, maybe 'happily ever after' just isn't in the stars.

Katerina headed out, leaving me at the sink to finish up, and I was just in the process of drying the last of the dinner plates, piling one on top of the other, when a familiar voice filtered into the room. I strained my ears, trying to work out who it could be. Of course, there weren't many Greek speakers I could pick out through sound alone, but on this occasion, it didn't take long at all to work out who the particular vocal belonged to.

Bugger! I immediately froze to the spot. *What's he doing here?*

I told myself that with a bit of luck Sam the Climber was making nothing more than a simple pit stop while en-route to some other more permanent establishment for the evening and in the meantime, all I had to do was stay quiet. Throwing the tea towel over my shoulder, I crept over to the cupboard, doing my utmost not to make any noise as I put the stack of plates back where they belonged, all the while wondering just how long I could get away with loitering out in the kitchen before any suspicions about my prolonged absence were raised.

'Lydia!' Katerina called out. 'Come and get some coffee!'

Bugger! Bugger! Bugger! Now there was no getting away with it.

I hadn't talked to Sam since that fateful night in the bar, so I still didn't know his exact position on my alleged occupation and as such my mind began racing with one question after another. Had he researched my identity on the internet as he'd suggested? Or had he not? Had he simply got waylaid checking his email account instead and in the end not got around to it?

That is feasible, isn't it? I was getting desperate. But I'd never been any good at second guessing and I realised that if I really did want answers, there was only one way I was going to get them.

I put the tea towel down, telling myself it wasn't important. Even if he did know the truth, he hadn't said anything to the Fatolitis and that was all that really mattered. *Just who is this man anyway?* I attempted to bolster my confidence. *So what if he knows you told a fib, what can he possibly do about it now?*

More to the point, this was the man who didn't just kick a football in your face, but somehow managed to turn you into a Billy Liar along the way as well, which means this is entirely his fault in the first place... Not exactly a great start to any relationship, is it?

I shuddered, realising what I'd just thought, although I obviously used relationship in its widest definition possible.

Feeling more in control, I took a deep breath and set a smile on my face ready for the fallout.

'Coming!' I yelled back.

And with that, I left the room determinedly.

'Sam.' I acknowledged him, maintaining a decidedly formal tone as I joined him and the Fatolitis family. 'How are you today?'

I could see he was amused by my stance and clearly more than happy to match my reserve.

'Very well, thank you,' he replied. 'Although I must say not quite as well as you by the looks of things.'

Whatever he meant by that, I ignored the jibe and took a seat, having already decided my best course of action would be to say as little as possible. That way I'd have a better chance at gauging what he did or didn't know and, at any rate, it wasn't as if my silence would be noticed—the Fatolitis' constant chatter would more than make up for it.

At least that would normally be the case. I waited for someone to say something, but no one actually did. Instead, everyone exchanged weird smiles as if waiting for one of the others to get the conversation going. Very strange behaviour considering they'd usually be talking nineteen to the dozen at this time, both verbally and with their hands. *Maybe it's because of their full bellies,* I told myself, although I knew that had never stopped them from speaking before. But, whatever the reason, the situation was fast becoming uncomfortable and the longer the hush went on, the worse the atmosphere got.

Katerina gave me a discreet nudge, accompanying this with a nod towards Sam—although I didn't see why it was my responsibility to entertain the man, especially when they knew him better than I did.

'What?' I mouthed.

She shook her head at me as if I was such a disappointment, although I didn't have a clue as to why. In fact, things were getting weirder by the minute and if I didn't know any better I could've easily mistaken the Fatolitis' consummate professionalism for visible relief when a couple of customers finally entered the premises.

Yiannis all at once jumped up from his seat. 'Time to get back to it,' he said.

Not that he was *really* making an overly hasty bid for his place behind the bar and naturally I was only imagining the 'thank goodness for that' look that momentarily swept across his face. Likewise, as every other Fatolitis family member very quickly made their excuses and followed suit, neither was it particularly the case that they, too, couldn't get away quick enough. *They've all simply got work to do.*

Suddenly finding myself stuck with Sam the Climber, I continued my resolve to say as little as possible. After all, still not knowing how much he had or hadn't managed to find out about me, the last thing I wanted was to drop myself in it again and after recent events I probably would. However, I couldn't be altogether rude and, sipping my coffee, I mustered a polite smile or two every now and then just to be courteous. But it seemed my refusal to talk didn't faze him at all.

He leaned back in his chair and stared at me with something of a disconcerting grin and the longer he held his gaze, the more uneasy I began to feel. 'They think we'd make a good couple,' he eventually said. 'That's what their odd behaviour's all about.'

I nearly choked on my coffee. 'Sorry,' I replied. I'd obviously misheard.

'The Fatolitis think we're well suited.'

I looked around at my hosts, mortified to find Maria and Katerina excitedly giggling as they observed Sam and me from afar, both of them whispering behind their hands. While Efthimeos stood there nodding like some proud father, clearly giving the two of us his blessing. In fact, all but Yiannis were giving us the thumbs up in one way or another. *Ah, the lovely Yiannis.*

'Like that's ever gonna happen,' I said, not sure whether it was actually the young barman or, indeed, Sam I was referring to.

'Oh, I dunno,' said Sam. 'Personally, I think they might have a point.'

I scrutinized his face, trying and failing to work out if he was being serious or not. 'So, it's a good job *I* have a say on the matter as well then, isn't it?'

The cheek of him. I inwardly fumed and continuing to drink my coffee. I realised this situation was getting me nowhere. I still didn't know what the man in front of me knew with regard to my real life and I wondered how much longer I would have to suffer his presence.

'So,' he said. 'What have you been up to these last few days? I haven't seen you around.'

Of course, on the surface this was a simple enough question. But there was something in the way he spoke that made it sound more loaded than harmless, telling me I probably couldn't take anything that came out of Sam's mouth at face value.

'Oh, you know,' I replied, doing my utmost to come across as breezily non-committal as possible. 'Lazing on the beach, trips down to Pothia, stuff like that…'

'And I see the Fatolitis have been taking good care of you,' he continued. 'Keeping you well fed.'

Unfortunately, this time I did choke, hot liquid exploding uncontrollably from my mouth and out through my nose. Attractive most certainly not, but, as I tried to locate a much-needed napkin to wipe up the subsequent spillage, I wasn't about to give him the upper hand completely.

'Yes, they've been very hospitable,' I spluttered, mopping myself up and calming myself down. I levelled him with a smile.

For all I was aware, he might still only be making idle chit-chat; people often do under these circumstances, don't they? And, having not done any internet investigations at all, Sam was now simply and innocently conversing about my supposed gastronomic investigations, still believing I was the chef I'd claimed to be... I crossed my fingers.

'Helping you too, no doubt?' he continued. 'With your research into local cuisine... that is why you're here after all, isn't it?'

My stomach lurched.

'Yes,' I replied. 'You could say that.'

He sat forward in his seat and leaned towards me. 'It's all right,' he said, cool as anything. 'You don't have to keep up the pretence. You've got nothing to worry about from me.'

Shit! Shit! Shit!

However, I'd never been one to give up that easily and I was determined not to go down without a fight. Furthermore, I knew from experience I could be very convincing when I wanted to be. All I had to do was stick to my guns long enough and Sam would eventually have to concede he had, in fact, got it all wrong and that I really was who I'd actually claimed to be.

I crossed my fingers even tighter.

'Pretence about what?' I asked, keeping up the façade. 'And why should I be worried?'

'Let's put it this way,' he replied. 'There's no restaurant going by the name of, what was it? Oh yes, Austen's. And there's definitely no chef going by the name of Lydia Livingston.' He sat back in his seat again, while I squirmed in mine. 'But, like I said,' he went on. 'Your secret's safe with me.'

It appeared I'd met my match and I had no choice but to reluctantly acknowledge the game was well and truly up. Not that I believed for one second he was about to just leave it at that. If that was the case, surely, we wouldn't even be having this discussion?

'What's the catch?' I asked. In the end, when it came to men like this, there was always a catch.

'There isn't one,' he simply stated, something I didn't believe for one second.

I waited for him to drop the bombshell... and then he hit me with it.

'There is a condition though,' he said. 'I want you to come on a date with me.'

'What?' I said, much to my embarrassment attracting everyone's attention as I struggled to keep my voice down.

I leaned forward, this time making sure to speak quietly. 'You mean you're blackmailing me into going out with you?'

'Unless you want me to tell the Fatolitis everything I know. Then yes, I suppose that's the crux of it.'

I couldn't believe what I was hearing. I mean, what kind of man had to stoop to such tactics in order to get a date? And he was being so blasé about it all, as if his bribery was a mere trifle.

'You wouldn't?' I said, throwing down the gauntlet.

He eyed me for a moment and I could see him deciding whether or not to call my bluff.

'Yiannis!' he suddenly shouted out, pushing things one step further in response to my challenge.

My eyes narrowed. And even though I still wasn't one hundred per cent convinced Sam was really about to drop me well and truly in it, I wasn't sure if I had the courage to risk letting him.

CHAPTER EIGHT

He who has no brains has legs.

As I made my way to the hotel situated at the edge of the village, a smart little place that opened its pool to residents and non-residents alike, I clicked the 'end call' button on my mobile. It was unusual that neither Mum nor Dad had been there at the other end to pick up, although I supposed it was probably for the best.

Under the circumstances, I wasn't really in the mood to talk to anyone, let alone listen to idle chit-chat. Due to me being a habitual chatterbox they'd have only sensed I wasn't quite myself anyway, which would then open the door for them to insist I tell them why. Given our family dynamics, naturally that was something I most definitely couldn't do. With my holiday seemingly going from bad to worse with each passing day, I just wanted to escape the world and forget about everything and everyone in it. A few hours of undisturbed peace were just what I needed.

'*Kalimera*… good morning,' called the receptionist as I arrived at my destination.

'Morning,' I automatically replied, though what was so good about it I didn't know. Although, as I passed through the foyer and headed towards the pool area, I was more concerned that there'd be at least one sunbed left on which I could park my sorry ass. Otherwise I'd just have to turn around and go straight back to the apartment.

I stepped out into the open-air ready to scan the line of wall-to-wall sunbeds in search of that one empty lounger located somewhere among them. Much to my surprise, however, rather than coming face to face with a mass of dedicated sun worshippers hogging the area, there wasn't another soul in sight, leading me to believe that this must be the establishment where all the night owls resided—the ones who drank until the sun came up and slept until it went back down. At least that's what I hoped, because that would mean I'd have the whole place to myself for as long as I wanted it.

My spirits lifted slightly; such tranquillity was just the ticket for a woman determined to escape her woes. Opting for a sunbed right at the water's edge, I told myself there was no better way of seeking solace than a morning's respite from reality in the quiet calm about me.

'This is more like it,' I said to myself, happily stripping down to my bikini before laying both my towel and myself down on the plastic sunlounger. *Maybe things are actually starting to look up.*

My optimism was short-lived though. Despite feeling the warmth of the sun as it caressed my skin, even that wasn't enough to maintain my conviction to *not* think about my worries; thoughts about the last few days' events were creeping in regardless.

Who in their right mind tells a blatant lie and thinks they can get away with it? Apart from me... And when they get found out, which most people who tell porkies invariably do... Who on earth then ends up being subjected to some sort of blackmail plot...? Again, apart from me? I sighed at the ridiculousness of it all. 'Honestly, you couldn't write it!'

I lifted my bikini bottom's waistline to check how the tanning process was going. I noted that unlike my blooming holiday it was developing quite nicely. Then, in something of a pig-on-a-spit-movement, I turned over onto my stomach to ensure an all-round even skin tone.

Once settled, I got straight back into my tragic deliberations.

And who does the man think he is anyway? I fumed. *Trying to coerce me into going on a date with him like that? Surely, he could've done what normal people do when they fancy someone and just asked me out? Even if it is pretty obvious to anyone and everyone I would've only turned him down flat...*

Well, if he thinks he's going to get away with it, he's got another thing coming. Nobody messes with Lydia and lives to tell the tale!

In fact, I thought I might not go at all.

A sudden commotion back in the hotel reception area cut into my bravado. 'Clearly new arrivals,' I surmised from their enthusiasm. It was either that, or the receptionist's chirpiness was catching.

I tried to eavesdrop on the excitement, but other than gleaning the party members were English like me, I couldn't actually make out what any of them were saying and I'd have put money on the woman working the desk not being able to either. They were all talking at once and I could imagine her smile fading as a result. *Typical of large families.* At least it was in my experience; the Livingstons were more than adept at not letting each other get a word in.

I shot up onto my elbows, perishing the thought.

'No, it can't be,' I said, my ears now straining somewhat in a definite attempt to decipher at least one individual voice. *Surely, they wouldn't have followed me all the way here?*

Turning up unannounced would be extreme even for them, I told myself, dismissing the very idea. *You're just being paranoid because of all the complications of this trip so far.*

I carried on listening, but all I could hear now was the rumbling of suitcase wheels as luggage was dragged along and off into the distance. The new arrivals were clearly in the process of being shown to their rooms and, shaking my head at the ludicrousness of any such concerns, I wrote off my suspicions as just plain daft. Instead, I snuggled back down for another bout of peaceful sunbathing; something I should've known wouldn't last.

It wasn't long before the eager pitter-patter of bare feet approached; an innocent enough sound, I realised, considering my location. But before I knew it, this simple pitter-patter was quickly replaced by an almighty chorus of the word 'Charge!'—a war cry that was, much to my horror and without warning, suddenly converted into an exceptionally loud 'Splash!'

'What the…?' I shrieked, leaping off the sunbed the second the resulting wave of water washed over me.

I immediately spun around, more than ready to give the rowdy blighters a very large piece of my mind. But, coming face to face with the offenders, I stopped dead in my tracks, the words for any such telling off suddenly refusing to come out.

We all just stared at each other speechless—me standing there like a drowned rat, them with their hands over their mouths desperately trying to stop themselves from laughing.

'Luke? Johnny?' I eventually said, still not quite sure if the two wide-eyed boys in the pool really were my two young nephews, or simply, *please God, I'll do anything if you make it so*, a pair of exceptionally good doppelgangers.

'Aunty Lydia,' they replied, immediately confirming my worst fears. 'How did you know we were coming?'

I remained frozen to the spot, at the same time wondering if I should just grab my stuff and cut and run, never to be seen again. As if things weren't complicated enough around here at the moment— did I really want my madder than mad family added into the mix? And a quick escape would certainly solve a lot of problems.

Please, this can't be happening to me, I silently bemoaned. Not on top of everything else.

Of course it isn't. I pinched myself in the desperate hope that none of what was taking place right now was actually real; it was all just some terrible nightmare on account of my having fallen asleep in the heat of the blazing sun.

'Lydia?' a female voice called out from behind me. 'What're you doing here?'

I closed my eyes and slowly turned around. Upon opening them again, I realised this wasn't, in fact, a nightmare at all; the only feasible explanation was that I must've died and gone to hell. Except to make matters worse, it appeared that if you go to hell, any fashion sense dies along with you.

'Mum?' I asked, face to face with the biggest, brightest, yellowest floppy hat I'd ever had the misfortune to clap eyes on. 'Is that you under there?'

'Who else would it be?' she replied.

Unlike mine, hers was a rather bewildering question, as despite my earlier suspicions she was still the last person on earth I'd have expected to see. In truth, it would have been less of a shock to hear the woman in yellow identify herself as the Tooth Fairy or, indeed, Mrs Santa Claus… but hey, that's just me.

My attention was momentarily diverted when Dad and Pete decided it was time for them to make their appearance. 'Jesus Christ…' And even though their arrival came as less of a bombshell considering who had come before, what a sight to behold it was.

For some reason Dad seemed to think he was either on safari or somewhere in the Australian Outback, what with him being dressed in beige Bermuda type shorts and matching shirt. What was more, all that was missing from his ensemble was a set of corks from his equally beige hat and perhaps a shotgun at his side in case a giant lion or two should jump out at us.

Pete, on the other hand, had undoubtedly gone for a completely different geographical source for his wardrobe inspiration and was clearly under the impression that Kalymnos was in some way linked to America's fiftieth state. That was if his exceptionally bright Hawaiian shirt was anything to go by, and, looking at the pair of them side by side, it was a spectacle I'd never before seen in my life and nor did I ever want to see again.

'What do you both look like?' I had to ask.

'Lydia?' said Dad. 'What're you doing here?'

I looked from him and Pete to Mum and back again, all the while wondering what was wrong with these people.

'Isn't that something *I* should be asking?' I replied.

Mum looked at me aghast. 'You didn't really think we were going to let you celebrate your birthday without us, did you? That just wouldn't be right.'

'But I told you,' I said. 'I'm not having one this year.'

'Exactly,' said Dad. 'And if Mohammed won't come to the mountain... and besides, we thought we'd kill two birds with one stone. It's about time me and your mum had a holiday, don't you think? And your birthday gave us just the excuse we needed.'

I knew I couldn't disagree on the holiday front; a break was something my parents most definitely deserved and should've taken years ago. But with all the complications in my personal life, I still wished they'd simply forgotten about my birthday altogether just as I intended and chosen a different destination at which to treat themselves.

'Of course, it would've been nice if Steve and Jill could've been here as well,' Mum continued. 'But they couldn't get the time off work... Still, at least the boys are here, eh?' She smiled adoringly at her two grandchildren.

'And no, Lydia,' she went on to hastily add. 'That is not a cue for you to start preaching about how Jill might've been able to make the trip had she not made the decision to become a working mother!'

Not that the thought had even crossed my mind in this situation, but now she'd mentioned it... Although as I looked to Luke and Johnny, currently trying to drown each other in the pool, a small part of me appreciated why in some cases going out to work would be preferable.

Once again, I found myself side-tracked thanks to the arrival of texting, tweeting Tammy and, surprise, surprise, she was too preoccupied with her mobile phone to even lift her head and say hello. Fascinating to watch, of course, but how anyone could walk and text without bumping into anything was quite beyond me. On the plus side though, her physical presence if nothing else did at least complete the Livingston family invasion party. Taking them all in at once it was a case of sod the Ottoman Empire, the Italians, the Germans and goodness knows who else... Kalymnos wasn't going to know what had hit it!

'But I told you,' I said, getting back to the matter at hand. 'I'm not celebrating my birthday this year.'

'Rubbish!' said Mum. 'You're just being melodramatic as usual. It's just a shame you've ruined the surprise,' she continued. 'Our plan was to settle in here, let the boys have a bit of a swim and then come and find you later on.'

I began to picture them turning up at the Fatolitis, who, in turn, would excitedly welcome the famous chef's family into their establishment, and suddenly felt the need to swallow.

My family thought I was barmy enough when I was telling the truth, so goodness knew what they'd think if my lies ever came out and the disappointment my hosts would, no doubt, feel too… Then there was Sam the Climber to consider and, even worse, our supposed date! I cringed when I thought about the mileage he'd be able to get out of this little twist in events.

Oh God, what would he expect in return for his silence now?

'How long are you here for?' I asked, thinking if I could somehow just manage the situation.

'Not long enough,' said Mum. 'But we didn't want to overdo it on our first trip abroad, did we, Dad?'

'Oh no, we didn't want to do that,' he replied.

'I did,' said Pete, taking his shirt off ready to join Luke and Johnny in the pool. His bare white frame resembled a bottle of skimmed milk. 'Ten days is nowhere near long enough.'

'Oh, I don't know,' I replied, trying to sound positive.

I watched him take a long run and jump straight into the water much to the delight of my squealing nephews, more concerned about keeping the Livingstons away from the Fatolitis than their having fun. But ten days was a long time to be under such pressure and even with a bit of creative juggling, I still wasn't sure I'd be able to pull it off.

But what choice do you have? My parents were now settling themselves down next to texting, tweeting Tammy under one of the umbrellas.

Organised as ever Mum began rummaging in her bag. 'Here, put some of this on,' she said, producing a jumbo-sized bottle of suncream and passing it to Dad. 'You don't want to get burnt on our first day.'

I smiled to myself; we were such a funny family. Mum the Matriarch, making sure the rest of us had everything we needed whether we liked it or not; Dad, happy to do her bidding because deep down he knew what was good for him; and then there was Pete, a big kid himself really, so he was quite at home getting stuck in with his nephews. And lastly, I supposed Tammy was just Tammy, with us in body if not in spirit. And yes, putting us all together, we might look like we were on leave from a mental institute, but, however unexpected, this was our first proper holiday together and one that I should be enjoying with them.

I let out a long guilty sigh for not appreciating the fact that they'd travelled all this way just for me and my birthday, that I was so important to them that they'd do all this in the first place. Instead, I'd shown more concern about my reputation than their efforts—a reputation that wasn't even deserved.

'What're you doing, Lydia?' asked Mum, interrupting my thoughts. 'Come and sit down.'

I raised another smile as I did what I was told and joined them, telling myself I had no choice but to put my selfish concerns to the side, even if it was only going to be for a few short hours. On balance, I needed to at least try and enjoy the here and now and not just for their sake, but for my own. After all, once they got wind of not just the lie I'd told but of the pretence I'd continued to uphold, they might never want to sit down with me like this again.

CHAPTER NINE

Whoever gets burnt by hot milk blows on cool yoghurt.

'Yes, if you just keep following the road,' I explained. 'Eventually you'll come to a sign saying "Argononta". The beach is on your left, you can't miss it.'

'And that's in English, is it?' asked Mum. 'The sign, I mean. Because there's no way me and your dad can read Greek and I doubt Pete will be much use. I sometimes wonder if he's capable of understanding his own language let alone anyone else's.'

'Yes, it's in English,' I reassured her.

'And you definitely don't want to come with us?'

Boy did I hate myself.

'No, honestly. Like I said, I'm not feeling very well so I'm better off here. Must've been all the excitement of your surprise arrival yesterday.' I tried to raise a laugh. 'It somehow knocked me out of sync.'

'Well what if I send everyone else off and I come and sit with you? I could bring you something?'

I should've known she'd suggest that.

'No, Mum, there's no point spoiling your day as well. I'll be fine on my own and I can catch up with you later. I'll probably feel better by then. You just go and enjoy yourself, yeah?'

'Well, only if you're sure?' she replied, although I could tell she wasn't convinced.

'I am sure. I'll speak to you when you get back.'

I ended the call hoping I hadn't sounded too eager in my desire to pack them all off without me and although I felt guilty for having to tell yet another untruth, in this instance I knew it was a case of needs must.

Then again, it wasn't even a lie, was it? It was more of an excuse. After all, their arrival had come as a bit of a shock and even Mum had said I looked a bit pale as a result. Thankfully, that had got me out of having to spend the evening with them, as well as giving me an alibi for today; I just had to get through the next few hours and then I could really focus on how best to handle things. Not that it was going to be easy.

I threw my mobile down on the nightstand, opened the wardrobe doors, and plonked myself down on the bed. 'What does a girl wear for a date she doesn't even want to go on?' I asked, staring at the line of neatly hung clothes.

I did toy with the idea of not going but thanks to the Livingstons' arrival that was no longer an option. I didn't have a clue as to what did or didn't constitute the perfect outfit for a blackmail victim, but I did know I wasn't about to get dressed up for the occasion. A man like Sam just wasn't worth the effort, although as I continued to gaze into the closet, I realised it wasn't as if I had it in me to dress down to the point of teaching him a lesson. To do so would be like showing my displeasure at being backed into a corner like this and attaching a degree of importance to this date, albeit in a negative way. That just wouldn't do. The last thing I wanted was for my coercer to think our rendezvous held any significance of any kind—good or bad.

Of course, it would've been easier if I'd have had some knowledge of the day's plan of action. As it stood, whatever I chose to wear could still turn out to be a big mistake. Yes, I'd packed my towel and bikini just in case we were off to the beach, as well as my book, thus giving me the opportunity to escape mentally if not physically; I just hoped that what lay in store didn't involve any form of climbing, although I wouldn't have put it past him.

A smile began to spread across my face.

'Climbing,' I said, at last coming to a decision, 'what better place to start from than that?'

I pulled out a simple white summer dress, convinced that alone would scupper the itinerary should the use of ropes and pegs turn out to be on the agenda. Let's face it, not even a man like him could expect me to shimmy up a rock face in a casual, strappy little number like that. And, coupling it with a pair of flat flimsy sandals just to make sure, I contentedly donned the ensemble, all the while looking forward to seeing the disappointment on Sam's face once he realised he'd have to come up with something else for us to do.

Not bad. I was pleased with how effortless my attire appeared, even if it had in reality taken some thinking about. 'Stylish yet at the same time understated. Nothing at all to send any message, one way or the other.'

A hollow beep sounding from the street below drew my attention to the window and I took a peak through the glass. *You've got to be kidding me.* I peered down at not just Sam, but Sam comfortably perched on a scooter of all things. And it wasn't even one of those smart Vespa or Lambretta models, I noted, it was one of those cheap run-around's that everyone rode about on.

He met my sickened gaze with a cheery little wave—a gesture I most certainly didn't appreciate.

'I don't know what you're smiling at,' I complained. 'Not only is this date a complete waste of my time and yours, I bloody well hate those things.' In fact, as far as vehicles went, in my view scooters weren't just downright dangerous, they also played havoc with a girl's hair—whether she did or didn't choose to wear the helmet.

Still, on a more positive note he wasn't carrying any climbing gear on his back, so at least I was off the hook there. However, that also meant I was no longer one step ahead when it came to spoiling his overall game plan, but I supposed rather that than finding myself halfway up a mountainside against my will.

God, I hate that man. I signalled I was almost ready.

Then I grabbed my bag to leave, locked the door behind me and begrudgingly sauntered down onto the street. At the same time, I told myself I was just going to have to grin and bear the next few hours, whatever they happened to bring.

'Good morning,' said Sam. He grinned, evidently looking forward to our date a tad more than I was.

'Is it?' I asked, making sure not to match his enthusiasm. 'Don't think I've had one of those since I first got here.'

He ignored my remark. 'Very nice, I must say,' he said instead. He looked me up and down appreciatively, before taking his rucksack off and placing it securely between his legs. 'Glad you thought me worth the effort.'

'No effort at all,' I replied, matter-of-factly.

'Although it might be an idea to change your footwear,' he added.

I looked down at my feet, secretly pleased. I'd chosen these sandals for a reason and my cunning plan was already working. Maybe this day was going to be a good one, after all. 'What, and ruin the overall effect?' I asked.

'Suit yourself then,' he said, at the same time offering me a helmet and starting up the engine. 'But don't say I didn't warn you.'

I climbed onto the back of the scooter, holding on to him. 'So where is it we're going?'

'You'll see when we get there,' he replied, although his lack of information didn't really come as any great surprise. Sam hadn't exactly proven himself to be the most straightforward of guys thus far, had he? I just hoped we weren't about to embark on anything too strenuous. 'But don't worry,' he said. 'I'm sure you'll like it.'

Despite his reassurances, as we headed out his response didn't feel all that comforting, his use of the word 'worry' being enough to make me do just that. Especially in the light of the last time he told me I had no cause for concern—a statement which was very quickly followed by a spot of blackmail. However, as we began following the long coastal road out to Emporios straight past the main climbing sector, a part of me couldn't help but feel a little disappointed. I'd been looking forward to a bit of verbal sparring when I refused to carry out Sam's mountainside bidding.

But then again, it did look a bit of a trek just to get to the base of the things, let alone being expected to make like Spiderman once there. So maybe he'd recognised the fact that a beachside village was a much better destination for a woman like me, more used to pavement pounding around a shopping centre than being stuck halfway up some mountain—the two of us clearly coming from different stock.

He flicked the indicator switch and we took a right turn.

Or maybe not!

Great! We began making an ascent up into what looked like the middle of nowhere. *I should've known things wouldn't be that straightforward.*

At least with Emporios there was only one route in and one route out, so if I needed a quick escape at any point I'd have known exactly which direction I should take. Now I wouldn't have a clue where to go and as we took this bend and that bend, all the while getting higher and higher, I started to feel like I was really at this man's mercy and in more ways than one.

As alarm bells go, though, I didn't get the chance to dwell on the verity that I was actually heading out into the back of beyond with someone I knew absolutely nothing about. Thanks to our increasing altitude, rather than panicking over what was to become of me in a 'stranger danger' kind of way, my uneasiness about heights began to take precedence.

The sheer drop to one side was terrifying and my body tensed all the more with each passing second. Automatically, I tightened my grip around Sam's waist—an action he no doubt loved, and I hazarded a guess this was all part of his ploy from the beginning. Still, on the plus side, if I were to fall to my death, so firm was my clutch he would definitely be coming with me—every cloud having a silver lining and all that.

'Try and concentrate on the scenery,' said Sam. 'Look into the distance.'

I think he was hoping that my doing so would lessen the stranglehold I had on his torso by now, as well as going some way to ease my mind. But even though the long-distance view was positively one of the best I'd seen on the island so far, my heart still raced and no matter how hard I tried to concentrate, my eyes still kept getting drawn to the plunging abyss.

'Not far now,' he said and this time he was, in fact, being earnest. Much to my relief, it wasn't long before we reached the summit and were at last beginning our descent.

I could feel my body start to relax and my pulse begin to slow along with the speed of the scooter. 'Why are we stopping?' I asked—we hadn't reached the bottom.

Then I understood.

It was one of the most bizarre things I'd ever seen: the tarmac just stopped, bringing our journey to a sudden and abrupt end, literally rendering us on a road to nowhere. We couldn't continue on two wheels even if we'd tried and in the space of a few minutes I went from anxiety ridden to utterly confused.

As we de-helmeted and disembarked, I looked about me, flummoxed not just in relation to our current whereabouts but also our intended destination.

'Come on,' said Sam, happily taking an obscure narrow dirt track that led away from the roadside. 'It's this way.'

Again, I looked around, unsure as to whether or not I should. There was no one else in sight and the only other track out of there was all the way back up the mountain and down the other side again, a hike I most certainly didn't want to do. I realised, though, that unless I wanted to stay where I was I had no choice but to follow his lead. *Talk about a no-win situation.* I awkwardly traced his steps.

The path was rocky and treacherous and as I stumbled along, all the while struggling to keep up, I wished I'd taken Sam's earlier advice and changed my shoes. The fact that I felt hot and bothered owing to the searing temperatures wasn't helping any, and my feelings towards Sam were getting increasingly bitter for putting me through all this. 'It's all right for you,' I grumbled. 'You're a climber. You're used to coping with this kind of landscape, whereas I'm not.' Not that I minded talking to myself, on account of him being way ahead of me. It somehow made the struggle easier.

There was a lot of faltering and stumbling on my part, until eventually we arrived at the grounds of a little chapel. 'Surely we haven't come all this way just to visit a church?' I asked, no matter how traditionally blue-and-white pretty it was. Although even that was preferable to the alternative and I felt even more wretched when I was forced to follow my guide as he made his way around the building's exterior and on to another dirt track beyond.

I refused to let myself cry.

'You all right?' he called back, stopping for a moment, I'm guessing to make sure I was still there.

'I would be if you'd just slow down a bit,' I replied. 'And also had the decency to tell me where it is we're going!'

He smiled a secretive smile that I wanted to knock clean off him, refusing to give up the tiniest of details before turning and continuing on his way.

'Effing bar steward!' I said, with absolutely no other option but to resume the chase. *The man's obviously a sadist.*

'Ouch!' A sharp pain shot through my ankle as I tripped over a perilously positioned rock. And with my face very quickly about to crash into the ground, I put my arms out to break my fall.

Sam raced back to my rescue. 'What happened? Are you okay?'

'Am I okay? Am I okay?' Of all the stupid questions! 'Do I look like I'm okay?'

He helped me back up into a standing position.

'First that bloody football and now this... What is it with you?'

I let him steer me over to some random giant boulder, surprised when in one swift movement he lifted me straight up and onto it, an action that would've been quite impressive if it had been undertaken by anybody else and if I hadn't been in so much agony.

'There isn't any real damage,' he said, gently checking over my foot. 'You must've just twisted it a bit.'

'That's easy for you to say,' I replied, grimacing. 'You can't feel how much it hurts.'

'Well, it's not broken, if that's what you're worried about.'

'Oh no... and you're a doctor now, are you?'

He paused in what he was doing. 'I'm a climber. Broken bones come with the territory.'

Whether it was the pain I was experiencing, the situation I was in, or a combination of the two, my resolve not to cry weakened and I felt tears beginning to flood my eyeballs.

Sam looked at me with such tenderness, I almost thought he cared. 'Look, why don't you wait here? Let me get rid of this...' He picked up his rucksack. 'And then I'll come back and get you.'

I gave a pathetic nod and wiped my eyes. 'But where are you going?' I asked.

'You'll see,' he simply said. 'I won't be long.'

I watched him continue along the rest of the track without me, and, to be honest, I was glad for the rest. 'Whatever this is about,' I shouted after him, trying to reclaim some of my earlier attitude. 'It better be worth it.'

Sitting there all on my lonesome, I took in my sun scorched, arid surroundings, realising my so-called date hadn't even had the decency to leave me a bottle of water. 'How do you do it?' I asked myself from my solitary perch. 'How do you get yourself into these muddles?'

Not that I'd ever found myself dumped on a big rock in the middle of a foreign land before, I had to concede, although as I took off my sandal to rub my throbbing foot, I supposed there was a first time for everything.

It felt like I'd been sitting there for a very long time when I finally spotted Sam making his return. 'And about blooming time,' I said, by now so bored even *his* company was better than no company at all. Nevertheless, this still didn't make me any more eager to jump down and start following him along that dusty track again, even if my foot allowed it. For one, I continued to feel way too sorry for myself to demonstrate any degree of enthusiasm, and two, I wasn't about to let him off with what he'd put me through anywhere near as easily.

'You ready?' he asked.

'That depends,' I replied, showing no signs of moving at all. 'On just how far we have to go.'

He lifted me off my station and our eyes met. Well, what else do you look at when someone's face is only inches away from your own? Suspended in mid-air it was as if an electric current momentarily passed between us, disappearing almost as quickly as it had appeared. I put it down to Sam feeling sympathy towards me—and so he should, all things considered, whereas I was just relieved to be off that damn rock.

'You can put me down now,' I said, which he duly did, seemingly embarrassed at keeping me airborne like that.

'Come on,' he said, taking my hand. 'It's just down here, I promise.'

By now, the fight in me had waned and I followed his somewhat careful lead as he physically guided me down the not-so-pedestrian-friendly trail. Quite the expert he was too, although I wasn't about to let him know that. If anyone needed a boost right now it was me and not him and that was exactly what I got; a little taverna came into view.

At last! An ice-cold beer was just what the doctor ordered. *We're here.*

Unfortunately, Sam just kept walking, which meant I had to keep walking too and as swiftly as my morale had risen, it just as rapidly plummeted again, courtesy of us completely passing the hostelry by.

How can he be so cruel? Fuming, I desperately tried to keep my frustrations hidden.

In fact, were it not for the baking sun I would have been half tempted to just plonk myself down on the ground in protest and undertake some form of sit-in.

Eventually, however, we came to the end of the trail. But, rather than experiencing any form of elation as we came to a standstill, I had yet one more reason to feel downright annoyed.

It was bad enough that I could hear waves lapping against the shore. After all, did the two of us really have to come all this way for a get-together on the beach? The sands of Massouri were practically on the doorstep of where this journey started! But worse than that was the high stone wall we were now face to face with, one I just prayed I wasn't expected to scale.

'Almost there,' said Sam, as if the obstacle in our way was nothing.

'You don't think I'm going to climb over that, do you?' I asked. 'Because if you do, you've got another think coming.'

'Now would I?' he replied.

I raised an eyebrow, telling him I wouldn't have put it past him.

'Don't worry,' he said, which under the circumstances was definitely the one word I didn't want to hear. 'The hard bit's over now.'

He took my hand again and led me along the wall.

'Where to now?' I asked. 'I don't know how much more of this I can take.'

Much to my relief, however, for the second time that day, Sam was actually being true to his word, as instead of hoisting me up and over as I'd anticipated, after a few short steps we came to a standstill.

He indicated to a conveniently sized gap through which I could squeeze. 'Here we are,' he proudly announced. 'Our final destination.'

CHAPTER TEN

Everything in its time and mackerel in August.

'What do you think?' asked Sam.

Having manoeuvred myself through the gap, I'd almost dreaded what I was about to encounter. After all, things hadn't panned out too well up to now, had they? Leaving me to think the next leg of our date would bring much of the same.

This, however, I hadn't expected.

I took in the white pebbled, bay-like cove, so beautiful and charming that words escaped me. It had to be one of the island's hidden gems, completely untouched by the vulgarities of modern-day tourism. No sun beds or umbrellas or the like, just a huge fallen tree to lean against and, apart from Sam and I, not a soul in sight. The only sound came from the gentle waves as they washed against the shore. I looked out to sea at the sun's rays glistening and dancing on the water's surface, and even from my position by the wall I just knew how clear the waters were. And the serenity of the place... it felt like an intrusion on nature just being there.

'I bet no one else has ever taken you to paradise before, have they?' he said, content to appreciate the view alongside me.

'Sorry?' I said, still too mesmerized to really listen.

'That's what the locals call it,' he explained. '*H paralia tou paratheisou*... the beach of paradise.'

'Well, it certainly lives up to its name,' I replied, all the effort and physical pain it had taken to get there now nothing but a distant memory. 'I've never seen anything like it.'

'Come on,' he said. 'There's more.'

He suddenly sprang into action, leading me around to the other side of the fallen tree, where much to my surprise he'd already laid out a picnic for us. There was salad, fresh bread, cheese, plus sliced meats and even a bottle of wine with a couple of glasses—the man had certainly excelled himself and, once again, I found myself speechless.

Nobody had ever done anything as sweet as this for me before and although I couldn't understand why he'd go to such lengths, it was fair to say Sam had actually put a lot of thought into today. *But why?* I looked from the picnic blanket to our environment and then to Sam and back again, feeling it was all a bit weird.

He must've sensed my uncertainty, his smile going from his usual confidence to faltering for a change. 'What?' he asked. 'Don't you like it?'

'Well, yes,' I replied. 'But I don't get it.'

'What do you mean?' He appeared almost hurt.

'Well, first you blackmail me, which even you have to admit is a bit creepy... a lot creepy really. And then you go and do all of this, which is... to be honest, under the circumstances, I'm not sure what it is.'

'Put it this way,' said Sam. 'Would you be here with me now if I hadn't coerced you into it?'

I shrugged. 'Probably not.'

'Definitely not, you mean. From the day I first clapped eyes on you, it was pretty clear you wouldn't entertain the likes of me.'

I thought back to that very first boat trip over, almost embarrassed at how judgemental I must've looked. 'You climbers are a pretty strange-looking bunch,' I said.

'There you go then. The blackmail was a means to an end. How else was I going to get the chance to show you what a nice guy I am, which is all I ever wanted to do?'

He seemed genuine enough, anxious I should believe him. But I still wasn't sure. 'Yes, well, don't you go getting it into your head that a bit of bread and cheese and a nice view is enough to let you off the hook. I'm still here through force and not choice, you know.'

He visibly relaxed. 'Shall we?' he said.

We sat down on the blanket and he poured me some wine.

'Aren't you having any?' I asked, accepting the glass.

'Strictly water for me, I'm afraid,' he replied. 'Someone's got to get you back safely.'

I scoffed. 'Well as long as that's all it is. Plying me with alcohol isn't going to get you anywhere!'

We fell into a moment's silence, absorbing the tranquillity.

'Can I ask you something?' Sam eventually said.

I sipped my wine. 'Depends what it is.'

'Why are you here? Really here, I mean? What brought you to Kalymnos?'

I sighed, not one hundred per cent sure how to answer or if I wanted to answer at all. If my own family didn't understand where I was coming from then how could a complete stranger, which was essentially what Sam was. And I already knew that compared to most women's ambitions, my one and only desire to live the fairy-tale 'happily ever after' wasn't just deemed childish in comparison, it went against what everyone viewed as the feminist grain—enough people had told me so over the years. It didn't matter how much of a conscious decision I'd made, how much of an assertion of my right to choose it had been, and it certainly didn't matter how seriously I'd taken it. In fact, it was of no consequence whatsoever that I'd put as much, if not more work, into my future as every other woman had put into theirs, yet people still refused to understand.

'You'll only laugh,' I said.

'Try me,' he replied.

I eyed him up, reasoning a man who'd gone to all this trouble just for little old me deserved some explanation after the lie I told, even if I wasn't convinced he'd fully get it. Then again, so what if he didn't? It wasn't as if his opinion on the matter counted for anything, did it? So what the heck.

I gathered my thoughts.

'You know all that stuff about this alleged "new" man we've been fed all these years? And about women having it all? The fantastic career, the perfect partner, two point four kids etcetera, etcetera… You only have to look at the lives of normal working women to see it's all a myth, that it doesn't exist. For most of them, it's more about juggling than it is plain sailing. At least that's what it's like in my world, and I didn't want that for myself.'

I could see he wondered where all this was going.

'Anyway, you're looking at a woman who refuses to take part in some impossible balancing act. Someone who decided to focus on family rather than work and who's spent years searching for that special someone who's happy to let her.' I let out a little laugh. 'She's made a career out of it, in fact… excuse the pun. Doing everything she can to make sure that when she does find him, he'll know just how special she is too… Or, should I say, that was the plan.'

His silence made me feel a tad self-conscious but I'd started so I told myself I may as well finish.

'Which is why she's here. Having never had the pleasure of actually meeting her Mr Right, she thought it was about time she tried her hand at something else. And in order to figure out what that "something else" is, she's giving herself a bit of time and space to think about things. Although I'm sure none of this makes any sense to you whatsoever.'

'It does actually,' said Sam, although I didn't believe him.

'Well, if that's the case, you're the first person on the planet other than me to get your head around it,' I said, 'because no one else can.'

'I am struggling with one bit though,' he admitted.

'Oh yeah,' I replied. 'And which bit would that be?'

'The lack of suitors out there all vying for your attentions.'

I knew he wouldn't understand.

'Now you're either taking the Michael,' I said, 'or you're just being kind.'

We began picking at the food.

'So, go on then, tell me,' Sam eventually said. 'Who would be your perfect man? Besides me, of course.'

'You!' I replied. 'I don't think so.'

I munched on a piece of celery, not sure I really wanted to get into it. It felt like I'd said too much already and besides, I had, after all, come to this island to get away from all my woes, to think about the future and not the past.

'Oh, come on,' he encouraged. 'You've already given me half the story, so you might as well tell me the rest. It's only right I know what I'm up against if I'm to prove I'm your Prince Charming?'

Sod it, I thought. *I'm probably never going to see him again anyway.*

'Well, naturally he would be handsome,' I began.

'Like me, you mean?'

His words were accompanied with a devilish grin and I found myself acknowledging he did have something about him today. However, I also realised this was probably down to the combination of the sun and wine suddenly affecting my judgement.

'Not exactly, no,' I replied. 'You have far too much stubble for my liking. Although to be honest, you've got way too much hair full stop. Look at it—it's almost down to your shoulders.'

'Ah, but I like the natural look,' said Sam. He ran a hand through his mane. 'And besides, if it's that much of a problem, a simple comb and a pair of scissors would easily sort it. So, if you really want to convince me I'm not the man for you, I'm afraid you're gonna have to give me something better than that.'

'Oh, that's the game we're playing, is it? I tell you what it is in a bloke I want and you tell me just how you happen to have it?'

'Yep. It's the only way you're going to take my advances seriously!'

'Okay then,' I said, more than happy to accept the challenge. 'He has to have intelligence. That one's a must.'

'Politics, religion, geography, whatever the subject, I know them all.'

'Of course, you do,' I replied.

I narrowed my eyes, attempting to come up with one of my more obscure prerequisites. 'Yes, but would you be prepared to sit and watch *I Married a Witch* with me every Sunday afternoon, just so I get my fix?'

Another smile spread across his face. 'Veronica Lake and Fredric March, 1942, if I'm not mistaken... Of course, I would.'

I stared at him, surprised he'd even heard of the film let alone knew who starred in it. 'How do you know that?'

'You're talking to a guy who's watched quite a few black and white oldies,' Sam confidently replied. 'And quite a few times, at that. My mum's a huge fan. She practically raised me on them. So, come on, what's next?'

'He doesn't necessarily have to be wealthy as such,' I continued. 'But he does have to be solvent.'

'I see,' said Sam. 'So, I'm not the only schemer around these parts, eh?'

'What do you mean by that?' I asked. 'There's nothing wrong with a girl liking her home comforts, especially if she's the one spending most of her time in the home like I'd be. And not only that, I want lots of children. Five to be exact, and children come with a hefty price tag! Which takes us to something else on my long list of requirements: A high you-know-what count.'

Sam almost choked on a tomato—that one always got them.

'I don't know what's worse,' he spluttered. 'The fact that you even have a list—or the fact that you've got the quality of a man's sperm on it?'

'Think of it in terms of an arranged marriage,' I said. 'Parents who choose their future sons-in-law probably have a good idea as to the kind of man they want for their daughters. I'm doing the same, except it's for myself.'

'Anyway,' I continued, at the same time getting back to the case in point. 'When I was growing up, there was only three of us kids, not five like I hope to have. And even with both my parents working, there was never enough money to go around. At least not for the extras. So, what little cash there was went on my brothers and me, meaning Mum and Dad never got to do anything or go anywhere as a couple. I don't want that for my relationship.'

'Fair enough,' agreed Sam.

He was such a good listener; I couldn't stop talking.

'You know, they'd never ever had a holiday until they turned up here. And here I am with you when I should be with them. But because of your ridiculous blackmail plot, I had to tell another lie and say I was sick so I could come here instead. Which of course they can't ever find out about because they'd be so upset you wouldn't believe…'

'What?' asked Sam, suddenly interrupting. 'Your mum and dad are here? Now?'

'I'm afraid so. Along with my brother, my niece and my two nephews, if you must know.'

'Great!' he said. 'I can't wait to meet them.'

'What? I don't think so, mate.'

He gave me a look as if to say different.

'Oh, no!' I insisted. 'Like that's ever going to happen.'

Me and my big mouth. When would I learn to just keep it shut?

'I'm telling you. They're here. We celebrate my birthday. And then they go.'

'Your birthday?'

Shit! Now I really had said too much.

'So when is it?' asked Sam.

'When's what?'

'You know what.'

'It doesn't matter. I'm not celebrating it this year.'

'You just said you were.'

'No, I didn't.'

'But…'

Enough was enough.

'Getting back to our original conversation,' I said, cutting him off. 'When I have my own family, I want us *all* to enjoy life. Not just the children.'

Sam took the hint, albeit reluctantly.

'So that's where my Prince Charming's earning potential comes in. It has nothing at all to do with me being a money grabber. It has to do with him being a provider.'

'I was only joking when I said that, you know.'

'Which obviously counts you out of the running,' I said, unable to resist. 'After all, I wouldn't have thought an odd job man would have the pennies for a woman like me with lots of offspring to cater for.'

'Odd job man?' he said, as if he didn't have a clue what I was talking about.

'That's what you are, isn't it? When you're not on a rock face pretending to be a web-flinging superhero?'

He continued to appear a bit perplexed by my line of questioning and I wondered if I'd got it all wrong.

'I saw you the other day,' I explained. 'When I was on the bus back from Pothia. You were in some fancy house on the top road above Massouri and I assumed you were doing some work for the people who live there or something.'

'Oh, now I understand,' he said, it all apparently becoming clear. 'No, I don't work for them.'

'Really? So, what were you doing there?'

Trying to make his residential status fit in with my list of criteria obviously took some thinking about.

'I'm house-sitting, if you will. The owners let me stay there whenever I'm in town.'

'So, you're like a caretaker then?'

'Yeah, that's one way of putting it.'

'Well that definitely takes you out of the equation then, doesn't it? In the ideal man stakes, I mean.'

For a moment, it looked like he was going to come back at me with something, but he must have realised he didn't have a leg to stand on and thought better of it.

'Game, set and match to me, then. Don't you think?' I smugly raised my glass and in something of a celebratory toast clinked it against his. 'Cheers!' I said.

'Cheers,' he replied, taking a sip of his water as I took a drink of my wine.

'Although I suppose it's only right you enjoy your victory,' he added, 'while you still can.'

I stopped drinking.

'What do you mean?' I asked, realising I should've known Sam wasn't the kind of guy to simply leave things at that.

'Oh, I don't know,' he teased. 'Just that you might find the "game", as you so eloquently put it, isn't quite over yet.'

CHAPTER ELEVEN

Good morning, John. I'm planting beans.

I stepped out of the shower just in time to hear my mobile phone bleep. A text from Mum, I expected, wrapping myself in a towel. No doubt wanting to confirm I now felt well enough for an evening get-together.

TONIGHT'S OFF it read instead. THE BOYS HAVE SUNSTROKE. SEE YOU TOMORROW.

Why am I not surprised? I dropped the phone on the bed. Admittedly, though, I did feel somewhat relieved that they'd had to cancel. I wasn't just tired from all the fresh air and a day in the sun; opening up to Sam about what had been driving me all these years had left me a tad drained. And the last thing I needed right now was a night of Mum and Dad trying to build up some excitement over the big birthday celebrations coming up and making a song and dance over what a great time we were going to have. An evening like that would tip me right over the edge.

Still, at least when they were talking about my birthday they weren't pestering to come here, I thought, and there were only so many excuses I could come up with. As understanding as it might be for them to want to check out my holiday abode, I couldn't risk them coming across the Fatolitis. Not until I'd sorted out the mess I'd got into, although quite how I was going to do that was still one of life's great mysteries.

I snapped myself out of it, realising I was being selfish again. The main thing here was that Luke and Johnny were sick. At least I hoped it was Luke and Johnny the text was referring to; I didn't want to imagine poor Mum having to chase either Dad or Pete down the beach desperately trying to top up their sunscreen, with the two of them thwarting her every move in the same way the boys had probably done.

Of course, everyone knew the twins were too much for her to handle—everyone except the woman, herself, that is. Not being able to control her own grandchildren was something Mum would never admit to. And it wasn't as if Pete was much help when it came to looking after them either; if anything, he only encouraged their behaviour. As for Dad, well, he was just Dad.

Maybe I should go and check on them? I started to feel guilty. As nice as it would be to just stay here and spend the evening lounging about in my PJs, Mum could probably do with some help and I am the poor boys' aunt.

A knock on the door interrupted my deliberations and, wondering who on earth it could be, I tightened up the towel I was wrapped in and moved to answer the door.

'Oh,' I said, surprised to find myself face to face with Sam. It hadn't been too long since we'd parted. 'What do you want?'

'I've come to take you out for a pre-birthday drink,' he replied—at the same time giving me the quick once over, and unashamedly so too.

I threw my head back, groaning at the mere suggestion. 'What is it with everyone? I've made it more than clear I don't want a fuss this year, yet nobody is listening.'

'Come on, Lydia,' he coaxed. 'Don't be such a misery guts.'

I looked him straight in the eye. 'And if I say no, is that when you resort to blackmailing me again? Anyway, I can't, I'm busy,' I said. 'The twins are sick, I have to go and check on them.'

'Really?' he said, his voice a touch too delighted for my liking. 'Sorry. Really?' he repeated, this time making sure to adopt a more sympathetic tone. 'In that case, maybe I should come with you.'

I should've known he'd been playing me; that he wasn't the accepting, understanding guy he'd spent most of the day portraying himself to be. Standing there like butter wouldn't melt when really, he was just a chancer, taking advantage of every opportunity that came his way to the point that even two poorly children were now fair game... I considered telling him I wasn't the fool he'd mistaken me for, to go and take a running jump. But the last thing I wanted was for him to start causing me more trouble and I definitely didn't want him meeting my family.

'One drink!' I said. 'One drink and that's it.'

He smiled. 'What more can a man ask for?'

I swung the door in his face while I went to get ready. Not that I was exactly in any rush about it.

'You took your time,' said Sam, when I eventually reappeared. 'Although looking at you now, the wait was worth it.'

'Yes, well,' I said, locking the door behind me. 'As long as you don't think I've gone to any effort for you.'

We made our way down to the Fatolitis and, once again turning into quite the gentleman, he showed me to a seat.

'A blackmailer with manners,' I said. 'Who'd have thought it?'

I spotted Maria in her usual seat and gave her a little wave. But instead of greeting me with her customary smile, she quickly jumped up out of her seat and more or less ran off into the kitchen. The woman clearly wanted to avoid me altogether and her actions felt as unnerving as extraordinary.

My stomach lurched at the possibility of her knowing the truth, a large part of me wanting to follow Maria's lead and flee—because when it came to showdowns, I liked to be prepared. *But she couldn't know, could she?* Apart from Sam, no one else was aware of my real identity and as far as I could tell, he was having way too much fun with my predicament to want to drop me in it.

I looked to him, regardless, for some sort of explanation, sure he hadn't told her about my little white lie. He shrugged, seemingly unconcerned.

'Now what can I get you?' he asked, instead.

Maybe I'd imagined it.

'Just a glass of wine, please,' I replied, half remembering the last concoction this man had delivered into my possession, yet still preoccupied with Maria's sudden need to escape.

'Red or white?'

'Red.'

I watched him head off to the bar before turning my attention to the other Fatolitis, wondering if they were hoping to steer clear of me too. But with Efthimeos busy with other customers, Katerina wiping down tables and Yiannis now deep in conversation taking our order, nothing else seemed peculiar in any way.

Then again, that just meant they were taking care of business, not necessarily that all was normal.

You're just being paranoid. After all, that is what happens to people who're less than honest, isn't it? The stress of having to keep up the pretence means they start to see things that aren't really there, something that was evidently happening to me now.

I reassured myself with the possibility that Maria had simply remembered she'd left a pan on the stove, a pan that without her immediate attention was in danger of burning, and I shook my concerns free.

'Come on, Sam,' I said quietly, willing him to get on with my drink. Surprising really, considering only moments before I hadn't actually wanted one.

I gave another cautious glance about my surroundings just to ensure all still appeared well, and this time I couldn't help but notice the number of females on the premises keen for Sam to go and join them. That was if their admiring glances were anything to go by, although what they saw in him was anyone's guess. As far as I was concerned, once he'd handed over the glass of house red, they were more than welcome to take him. The man was too much of a game player for me, even if he could be quite charming with it. And funny, I supposed, thinking back to today's date; slightly handsome, even, when the light was right. But most of all, he was definitely intriguing.

'*Kalispera!*' A high-pitched voice suddenly called out, causing me to turn along with everyone else to see who it belonged to.

Wow… I thought, spotting the newcomer. As grand entrances go, this woman certainly had hers down to a tee.

She didn't walk; she shimmied, making sure to give a suggestive wink to the odd unsuspecting male as she made her way through to the bar. Although her confidence was well deserved considering how stunning she looked, what with her perfect hair and designer clothes, the less charitable side of me thought it was just a shame she didn't have the class to go with it.

I watched on as the Fatolitis greeted her with open arms and despite my failing to understand any of the conversation, it was obvious they all knew each other well by the looks of things. And that included Sam judging by the way the two of them were now throwing their arms around each other.

'It's great to see you again, Soulla,' said Sam, at last letting go.

She replied in Greek, her arms gesticulating all over the place. And her voice was so penetrating I was concerned that each and every glass in the establishment was now in danger of shattering.

Don't mind me. I wondered if I should just leave them to it. Not that I was feeling left out or anything—now I just wanted my drink.

Sam eventually landed back at the table, bottle of beer in one hand and the biggest glass of wine I'd ever seen, filled to the absolute brim, in the other. Doubtless to compensate for the fact that he'd abandoned me.

'Well, you did say you were only having the one drink,' he explained. 'So I thought it only right we make it a large.'

I took the glass and he took a seat.

'A good friend of yours, then?' I asked, indicating to the mystery woman now deep in conversation with Katerina.

'Not really,' he said. 'Just someone you don't want to cross.'

The two of them clearly had a history.

'It's not what you think,' he said.

Like it mattered to me one way or the other.

'So, what are your plans for tomorrow?' he asked, swiftly moving on.

I tried to stop myself from grinning. It was nice to watch him doing the squirming for a change.

'Oh, I don't know,' I replied. 'A relaxing day at the beach would've been nice. But seeing as I'll be spending it with the family, I doubt very much that's on the cards. The Livingstons don't do calm and serene.'

'My kind of people,' said Sam.

'Which is easy for you to say,' I retorted. 'You haven't met them.'

I cut him off before he suggested he might join us. 'So, what's your family like? Do you have any brothers or sisters?'

'Nope, I'm an only child I'm afraid. It's just me and my mum and dad.'

I saw him giving a quick nod to someone behind me, knowing that for some strange reason I wasn't supposed to notice.

'Would've liked them though. Your lot sound great fun.'

'That's one way to put it, I suppose.'

Suddenly the bar stereo struck up and a cheesy version of 'Happy Birthday to You' began blaring out, full blast. My eyes widened in horror. 'Please tell me this isn't for me,' I pleaded, mortified at the mere prospect. Too scared to look around just in case it was, I caught sight of Maria through the corner of my eye, making her way out from the kitchen carrying what had to be the most calorific of giant cakes, complete with one single burning candle sticking out of it.

My cheeks burned with embarrassment as she neared the table, everyone in the establishment now not just looking my way, but also joining in with the lyrics. And as the Fatolitis all gathered around me, the song at last coming to its natural end, everyone began to cheer the house down and I was forced to smile and play along.

I took a deep breath and much to everyone else's delight blew out the candle.

'Happy birthday, Lydia,' cheered Efthimeos through his giant, happy grin.

'Why did you keep this from us?' asked Katerina.

'Instead of leaving it to him to tell us,' said Yiannis.

I gave Sam a short yet accusing glare as Maria offered me a knife.

'You made this yourself?' I asked, accepting it.

She was confused by my words and Yiannis had to step in to translate.

'Yes, yes,' she beamed, at the same time nudging me to just get on and cut it, which I duly did.

As uncomfortable about the whole thing as I felt, I made sure to give the cake maker the first slice to show my gratitude. Just because I was furious at Sam for ignoring my assertion that my birthday would not, indeed, be celebrated this year, wasn't to say I didn't appreciate her effort. More to the point, it was such a relief to know that she hadn't been avoiding me earlier at all, but had simply rushed out of the way to put the finishing touches to her deliciously tempting masterpiece.

'This looks so nice,' I said, sharing the rest out with everyone else, of course making a point of leaving Sam until last, despite his protests.

The Fatolitis' phone began to ring and Katerina toddled off to answer it while we all tucked in.

'This is delicious, Mar—' I began.

My words were cut short when Katerina suddenly started shouting, her fork-tongued tirade silencing not just me but eventually the whole bar. On and on her angry rant went, leaving the rest of us too scared to breath yet able to share the odd questioning look, as we all wondered what on earth it was about. The tense atmosphere became tangible, until finally there was nothing else for it and the furious young woman slammed the phone down.

The rest of the Fatolitis rushed to her aid and, as I watched her look at her mother before bursting into a fit of distress-filled tears, I knew there was only one thing that could affect the poor girl in such a painful way.

'The wedding?' I anxiously asked Sam, hoping to God the groom hadn't just pulled out.

'I think so,' he replied. 'She did say something about the venue.'

'What? As in they're not gonna host it now?' I asked, although it would be fair to say a problem with the venue had to be better than a problem with the husband-to-be. 'Surely not, not at this late stage?'

The two of us sat there in silence, neither of us knowing what to say or do next.

'Do you think we should leave?' I whispered. 'Go somewhere else.'

Sam nodded, but before we were even out of our seats Yiannis had rejoined us.

'It's the reception,' he explained. 'They've double booked.'

'But the wedding's only a week away,' I replied. 'And they've only just realised?'

'Tell me about it. Although why did they cancel Katerina's party and not the other one?' He turned his attention directly to Sam and they finished the exchange in Greek. However, Yiannis's increasingly frustrated tone gave me the gist of what he was saying.

I couldn't blame him, of course. I'd be fuming too. This was, after all, the most important day in Katerina's life so far and it didn't take a brain surgeon to imagine what his sister was now going through. Heck, what the whole family was going through.

'Can't you hold it here?' I asked, desperate to come up with a solution.

Both Yiannis and Sam fell silent.

'You have the space,' I continued, taking a quick glance around. 'And with the right tables and decorations it would make a beautiful place to hold a wedding reception!'

My proposal took a moment to sink in.

'It's just a suggestion,' I said. 'But you're probably right. It's a silly idea.'

Without warning, Yiannis raced back over to his family and was once again speaking nineteen to the Greek dozen. But whatever he said was enough to stop poor Katerina from crying, each of them now listening to every word coming out of his mouth.

Their concerned frowns began to relax, eventually morphing into smiles.

'Bravo! Bravo!' cheered Efthimeos, suddenly charging in my direction. He hauled me up onto my feet and kissed my cheeks. 'Lydia!' he exclaimed. 'You are... you are a...'

'Genius,' called out Yiannis.

I sat back down in a bit of a daze, feeling Sam reach over and squeeze my hand.

'You are, you know,' he said. 'That was a brilliant suggestion.'

At last, I'd finally done something right.

Though while everyone else thought I'd come up with the perfect answer to Katerina's dilemma, the bride-to-be appeared less convinced. She began speaking, again in Greek, so again I was at a loss. While everyone else listened to her apprehensions, all I could do was wait until some sort of clarification was forthcoming. Everyone's eyes once again turned to me, once she'd finished what she had to say.

'What?' I asked, instantly anxious.

Sam had obviously understood every single word of it and I could see him almost cringing.

Now I felt really, really nervous.

'What?' I asked again. 'What did they say?'

He screwed his face and closed his eyes as he spoke. 'They want you to do the food,' he said, before opening them again.

My eyes did the opposite and widened in horror.

I thought back to my lie about being a chef, to how I'd noshed the gastronomic gift left on my apartment patio and the subsequent meals I'd been sharing with the Fatolitis family ever since—all in the name of non-existent research—and in that moment, I felt utterly helpless. How on earth was I going to say no after all of that?

'But I've never cooked Greek food,' I said, squirming, in the frantic hope this would be enough of an excuse.

I waited, hopeful, while Katerina began her serious mutterings once more. Then she instructed Sam to translate her words.

I don't know who looked more desperate, him or me?

'She says you can make English dishes,' he said. 'Like the ones you make in your restaurant back home.'

I looked from Sam to Katerina, from her to the rest of the Fatolitis and then to my birthday cake and back again... And unable to muster up quite the right words, I found myself gulping, swallowing so hard it actually hurt.

CHAPTER TWELVE

The day sees the deeds of the night and laughs.

The doorbell rang, but instead of getting up to answer, the best I could muster was a long, self-pitying groan. Despite actually having been awake for quite a while I was damned if I was going to respond; my position under the bed clothes was far too safe a place right now.

My mouth felt as dry as a desert flip flop, my head was banging and there was a distinct risk that if I moved I might throw up—all the result of having drunk way too much the night before, a fact I now regretted. The celebratory beverages in honour of Katerina's wedding and my birthday had been flowing and I'd taken full advantage of anything and everything alcoholic on offer. Although when I say celebratory, for me personally, it had been more a case of drinking to forget about these two events... and, of course, forget I did. Forgetting had seemed such a good idea at the time, an idea for which I was currently paying the price.

The doorbell rang again, but I still refused to budge, telling myself that if I ignored them long enough, whoever was out there would soon get the message and go away. Besides, if it was that important, they could always come back later.

Everything went quiet. At last, I could relax...

Bang! Bang! Bang!

'What the...?' I jumped out of my skin, the door's *ding dong* suddenly replaced with the hullabaloo of all-out hammering.

'Please go away,' I pleaded, and the world being far too noisy and uncomfortable for me to even consider rejoining, I wrapped one of my pillows around my head in an attempt to block the racket out.

But still the Bang! Bang! banging continued.

It was clear whoever had come calling wasn't about to give up any time soon, leaving me no option but to reluctantly fumble for my dressing gown as I finally dragged myself out of bed. *Some people can be so inconsiderate.*

I cringed, my stomach churning and my skull cracking with every painstaking step as I made my way out to the kitchen. *Why, oh why, did I do this to myself?*

Bang! Bang! Bang!

'All right, all right,' I called out, even the sound of my own voice ricocheting around my cranium.

Bang! Bang! Bang!

At last I got to the door and opened it.

'Jesus!' said Sam, taking in the state of me. 'You look terrible.'

'And a good morning to you too,' I replied.

I turned, leaving him to let himself in as I crept my way over to the kettle.

'Here, you sit down. I'll do that,' he said.

I didn't need telling twice and immediately headed for a seat at the table. 'Don't suppose you've got a neck brace on you, have you?' I asked, convinced my head couldn't withstand any more movement.

'Self-induced,' he replied. The man was a monster.

I watched him busy himself making coffee, wondering if he really had to make so much noise. Then again, he was probably doing it on purpose anyway; not only did he seemingly get a kick out of terrorising me at every available opportunity, he'd made it quite clear last night that he wasn't impressed.

'So,' he said, placing a steaming hot cup in front of me. Then he took the seat opposite; in my view, this is never a good sign.

'So,' I replied.

We continued to sit in silence, although it was pretty obvious even to a sick woman like me that he was getting ready to say something. No doubt wanting to talk about the previous night's events, regardless of the fact that I felt in no condition to discuss the weather, let alone anything so serious.

Five, four, three, two, one...

'About last night,' he began.

I let my head slump forward, immediately wishing I hadn't.

'You can remember last night, can't you?' he asked.

His eyes burned into me and I raised my head again, this time making sure to do it more slowly.

'I don't want to talk about it,' I said. 'I'm feeling too sick.'

I gave him my best puppy dog eyes; however, despite my fragile state, the man was completely devoid of all sympathy. He just looked back at me, determined not to let the issue drop.

'Look,' I said, trying to gather enough strength to fight my corner. 'You saw the state Katerina was in as much as I did. How upset she was. What was I supposed to say?'

'You could have told her the truth.'

'Oh yeah, and that would've gone down well, wouldn't it? Sorry your wedding plans are falling apart, Katerina, but guess what? I can't do anything about it because I'm not really who I say I am.'

'You could've made something up. Which, let's face it, is something you've been good at up to now.'

His words stung; the hurt hung in the air between us.

'I'm sorry. I shouldn't have said that.'

'No. You shouldn't.'

Still, at least he had the decency to look like he meant it.

'But it's is her wedding day we're talking about here, Lydia...'

'Don't you think I know that,' I replied. 'I just wanted to help and when they put me on the spot...'

'This isn't about you though, is it? It's about her. And imagine how she's gonna feel when the whole event's ruined because you of all people agreed to do the catering.'

I knew he was right.

'What do you mean?' I asked, regardless. 'Me of all people?'

'Well, have you ever done anything like this before?'

My silence said it all.

'Can you even cook?'

Again, I said nothing.

'Jesus, Lydia…' He put his hands over his mouth and I could see he was taking a moment to think.

'You're gonna have to tell her you can't do it,' he said, pulling himself together. 'That she'll have to find someone else.'

I felt embarrassed at my stupidity. I'd supposedly come to Greece to sort my life out and I'd ended up doing anything but. It was more complicated now than it had ever been and all because of a foolish little white lie. One that I'd actually been silly enough to think I could get away with. And not surprisingly, me being me, I couldn't just leave it at that, I had to go and make things twice as bad. In not wanting to upset anyone my untruths were no longer just my problem, I'd made them someone else's problem too. Not a great predicament to be in.

Tears sprung from my eyes as I realised more than ever Sam was right; I should come clean. But if only it was that easy.

'You're just being a hypocrite,' I said, desperate to dismiss my own inner voice let alone his.

'Oh, I see. I'm the bad guy now, am I?' said Sam, almost laughing.

'Yes, you are,' I snivelled. 'First you blackmail me into going out with you and then you come here throwing your weight around. That's what good people do, is it?'

'Oh, come on,' he said. 'That's different.'

'Why? Because it's you? Because you being less than honest is different to me being less than honest?'

'I'm not saying that.'

'No? Then what are you saying?'

None of this was getting us anywhere. Sam still wanted me to come clean and I still didn't.

'Go on then,' he said, finally breaking the ensuing silence. 'Tell me. What's the alternative?'

I felt a glimmer of hope. Maybe he'd help me come up with some other solution.

'I don't know yet,' I replied, trying to sound confident. 'But I'll think of something. You'll just have to trust me.'

He looked me directly in the eye. 'Trust you?'

I couldn't blame him for mocking. If I were in his shoes, I'd probably do the same.

'Lydia, the Fatolitis are good people,' he said. 'They don't deserve this.'

'I know they're good people, Sam. They've treated me like family ever since I got here... But the way you're going on anyone would think I'd meant for all this to happen. For everything to get so out of control...'

'Then take control back,' he suggested. 'Tell the truth.'

Again, that was easy for him to say and again, it was hard for me to hear.

'Christ,' I said, feeling very sorry for myself indeed. 'Can things get any worse?'

Just then, my mobile began to ring.

CHAPTER THIRTEEN

**If you do not praise your own home, it will fall on you and
squash you.**

'Of all the gin joints, in all the towns, in all the world…'
Sam's impression of Humphrey Bogart might not
have been very good, but I did have to concede the man
had a point. Out of all the places they could've stopped off at for
their liquid refreshments, why, oh why, did the Livingstons have
to choose the Fatolitis?

We stood at the bottom of my apartment steps, peeking out
from behind a blaze of bougainvillea, trying to get the lie of the
land before making a move.

'Where do you think the Fatolitis are?' asked Sam.

I could feel his breath on my neck as he spoke and I noticed
his aftershave didn't smell at all bad. Although with my stomach
doing a little summersault I guessed it must be one of those cheap
concoctions—they always did have a habit of turning my tummy.

'Because you're going to have to tell them the truth at some
point,' he carried on. 'And sooner rather than later by the looks
of this.'

With a raging hangover and a dodgy stomach, I had hoped to
find just one or two of my family members in sight; but no, much
to my detriment they were all present and correct. Mum and Dad
were enjoying a nice cup of tea; Pete, not surprisingly, preferred a
beer; Tammy was, as usual, preoccupied with her mobile phone;
and although I couldn't actually see Luke and Johnny, they were
definitely around somewhere because I most certainly heard them.

'I know,' I replied. 'But I can't do it yet, can I? Not with this lot here. I need to get them all out of the way first.'

'And what if they already know? What then?'

'What do you mean?' I asked, this being the last thing I wanted to think about.

'Well, I don't suppose there are many Lydia's around here, are there? It only takes one family member to mention your name and the others would easily realise it's you they're talking about.'

I tried to ignore my rising panic.

'If that's the case I'll have to just handle it, won't I?' I said, in the meantime praying things hadn't got that far.

We carried on peeking.

'You can go, you know,' I said. 'There's no reason for you to stay.'

'What? And miss out on all the action? Miss out on meeting your family? I don't think so.'

Despite his bravado, I got the sense he felt as nervous as I did and in deciding I needed to get this out of the way for both our sakes, I took a quick glance around, relieved to find there still wasn't a single Fatolitis in sight. With a bit of luck, I'd be able to get the Livingstons to down their drinks and be off the premises before any of the family reappeared. And with even more luck, nobody would be any the wiser.

'I suppose the quicker I get this over with, the quicker we can relax,' I said, crossing my fingers that the two families hadn't already made some sort of connection. If my lot were going to find out about the mess I'd got myself into, I much preferred it was through me. And ditto when it came to the Fatolitis.

Although what I really, really wanted was for none of them to find out about my misdemeanours at all, or at least not yet; the odds of which were getting less and less favourable as time went on.

'You're not to say a single word,' I instructed. 'I mean it, Sam. Let me do all the talking.'

'So, I can't even say hello? That'll look a bit rude, won't it?'

I gave him one of my best stern looks.

Of course, I should've realised Sam hadn't been nervous at all, he'd just been lulling me into a false sense of security; either that, or he genuinely was keen to meet my family. A point made clear when, as I took a deep breath and stepped forward, putting on what I hoped was a convincing smile, he was already in the process of overtaking me.

'The Livingstons, I presume,' he said, making a beeline straight for them. Talk about corny. 'How lovely to meet you all.'

Watching him in action, I felt powerless. What did he think he was playing at?

'Lydia's told me so much about you,' he continued. Then he turned to me and smiled. 'Haven't you, darling?'

I'll give you darling!

If looks could kill, Sam would've died on the spot. He was evidently insinuating we were involved in some kind of holiday romance—a romance I was in no position to deny for fear of him dropping me in it. I looked to the Livingstons and as demonstrated by their shared raised eyebrows and impressed smiles I could see they believed him. Boy was he going to pay for this.

'Er, yes,' I replied, telling myself I had absolutely no choice but to play along. 'Mum, Dad, everyone… This is Sam.'

The men of my family rose to their feet.

'Pleased to meet you,' said Dad—although why he was employing the same formal tone fathers usually reserve for potential sons-in-law was anyone's guess. 'Any friend of Lydia's is a friend of mine.'

I cringed, realising it was probably wishful thinking on my father's part, given my history in the love department.

'Likewise,' said Pete, next in line, at the same time throwing me one of his cocky, knowing smiles; one that I could've slapped him for, the idiot he was. 'No wonder you've been keeping such a low profile, eh?'

I watched on, squirming as Sam smoothly turned his attention to my mother.

'*Kalimera*,' he said, showing off his Greek skills. 'You must be Lydia's younger sister?' He moved in to kiss both her flushing cheeks and even without the delicate tummy I could've vomited.

But then again, Mum had always been easily impressed. Unlike Tammy, I have to say, who hadn't even bothered to look up throughout all of this. Way to go, Tammy!

Mum let out a schoolgirl giggle. 'Please,' she said, 'call me Margot.'

'Margot it is, then. Now what can I get you?' He clasped his hands together. 'Another drink, everyone?'

What? They can't have another drink! That would mean bringing out one of the Fatolitis and then I'll really be up the creek!

The man had evidently forgotten we were on a mission here, one that involved getting rid of the Livingstons, not socialising with them.

Unfortunately for me, however, as soon as Sam's words were out, Pete was already answering. 'Well, I'll have another beer if you're...'

'No!' I quickly interrupted, not that I intended to sound quite so desperate in my attempt at regaining some ground. I adjusted my tone accordingly. 'I mean, I'm sure we're all fine as we are... aren't we? And besides, don't you have things to do today, Sam?' I fixed him with a charming yet menacing smile, willing him to take the hint and disappear or else.

'Oh yes, sorry,' he said, thankfully recognising a threat when he saw one. 'I forgot.'

'Oh, don't be so awful, Lydia,' said Mum. 'We're not in any rush, are we? And I'm sure whatever your gentleman friend has to do it can wait a little bit longer, can't it? Now come on, sit down, the pair of you.'

She indicated to the seats next to her and I reluctantly did as I was told. But not without throwing Sam a loaded glare first; one that only intensified when like any alleged doting partner, he proceeded to gently rest one of his hands on my knee.

I leaned into him, speaking through severely clenched teeth. 'You really are beginning to push your luck now.'

'Ah… young love,' said Pete, thankfully having never mastered the art of lip reading.

'Leave them alone,' said Mum. She turned to us. 'I think it's sweet.'

If only she knew.

'Here for a holiday are you, Sam?' asked Dad. 'Having a bit of time off from the day job?' Sadly, subtlety had never been one of my father's strong points and it was clear to all concerned that what he really wanted to know was what the man actually did for a living and how much he got paid.

'Something like that,' said Sam, leaving it there.

I couldn't help but smirk. So now he wanted to play ball and keep schtum; for some reason this was better than admitting he did odd jobs to earn his keep! Still, in the bigger scheme of things, I realised the less conversation that took place, the quicker we could get off. Although at this rate, it felt like we were going to be there all day.

'So, where is everyone, I wonder?' I asked—part of me thinking to be forewarned is to be forearmed, another part of me thinking this might be an inroad to suggesting we move on to somewhere else. 'It's not like the Fatolitis to stay out of the way.'

'Oh, you know this place, then?' asked Dad.

'There was an older gentleman here when we arrived,' interrupted Mum.

Phew, that got me out of answering that one.

'But he had to nip out. He said something about wedding plans and having to go and collect his family, I think.'

'Wedding plans?' I asked, nervous.

'Something like that. But to be honest, I couldn't really understand his accent.'

Double phew!

Although that probably meant they were on their way back by now and I seized the opportunity while I still could. 'There's no point us hanging around here then, is there?' I said, rising to my feet. 'They could be gone a while.'

'I have to say,' Mum carried on regardless, 'they're very trusting these Greeks, aren't they? Not at all like people back home.'

I sat back down again.

'That's because in the UK the till would've been robbed by now,' said Pete.

'Probably,' agreed Sam.

'Speak of the devil,' said Dad.

I followed his gaze to the roadside, half expecting to see a man in prison clothing carrying a bag of swag. Instead, I found myself almost squealing at the sight of the Fatolitis pulling up in their car. Now what was I going to do?

'Sam,' I said. 'Could I have a word with you please?'

'Oh, aye,' said Pete. 'What's all this about then?'

With no time to come up with an answer, I knew it appeared a bit odd that I stole him away like that. But it was a case of needs must and I quickly dragged him out of earshot.

'What're we gonna do?' I asked, frantic.

'What do you mean, we?' he replied.

'Oh no,' I said. 'You're not getting out of this one scot-free. I could've had them up and out of here in seconds if you hadn't jumped in.'

I decided to fight fire with fire.

'And besides, you're up to your neck in this as much as I am… I mean, the Fatolitis finding out I haven't been as upfront as I should've been is one thing, but what do you think they're gonna say when they realise you've been in on it the whole time as well?'

I could see the penny dropping.

'Exactly,' I continued. 'They're not going to be too happy, are they? Which is why you should've just helped me get rid of my lot when we had the chance, instead of us having to now stand here trying to come up with some sort of plan.'

I could hear the Fatolitis getting out of their car.

'Come on, Sam. You're good at this sort of thing. Quick, think of something!'

'We'll just have to try and keep cutting them off,' he said. 'Any mention of the wedding and we change the subject.'

'What? That's it?'

'Unless you can come up with something better?'

I supposed it was as good a plan as any at this late stage. 'And we get the Livingstons out of the way asap?'

'And once we've done that, you come clean to the Fatolitis?'

I bit my lip.

'Agreed,' I said.

There was no way I wanted to go through all this again; my nerves just wouldn't be able to take it.

We stepped out from our corner just as the Fatolitis made their entrance, bringing with them their excitable chatter and a shed load of shopping bags. Even Tammy looked up, disturbed by all the commotion, an action that was practically unheard of.

'Lydia,' said Efthimeos, arms outstretched ready for a hug.

'Oh, Lydia,' echoed Katerina, pushing in front of her father for first dibs. 'My darling, my saviour!'

Why did she have to be so dramatic?

She threw her arms around me, much to my family's dismay. Leaving me no choice but to discreetly shrug and pretend I didn't have a clue as to what the girl was referring to.

'You will come tonight, won't you?' she said.

This time there was no pretence. I really *didn't* know what she was talking about.

'To my engagement party,' she explained. 'I lay out my beautiful dress, veil, tiara, and shoes. We cover everything in rice and people throw money on them. Then we celebrate.' She chuckled. 'Again.'

For everyone's sake, I wished the family would just continue their way straight through to the kitchen but, alas, they didn't. Even Yiannis made a point of stopping.

'I didn't think we'd see you two today,' he said, laughing. 'Not after last night. It was fun though, eh?'

It was all getting way too close for comfort and I could feel another slight panic beginning to set in as a result.

Mum gave a loud, expectant cough and I looked to Sam, both of us aware that now came the dangerous part.

I steeled myself. 'Everyone,' I said. 'I'd like to introduce you to my family.'

The Livingstons all rose to their feet ready to be received, including Tammy, which almost floored me. So, mesmerized by the loveliness that was Yiannis, her mobile had been flung on the table—who'd have thought she had such good taste?

Efthimeos hugged and kissed them all, leaving my dad and brother a little shaken by the experience and my mum a little flustered by the all-encompassing welcome. Then he put his hand on his heart. 'Your daughter,' he said with sincerity, 'is my daughter.' He signalled to the rest of the Fatolitis to take their turn and the next round of hugging and kissing commenced along with the introductions.

'You've obviously made an impression,' said Mum proudly. She always did like a good fuss.

'I'll say,' said Dad.

Pete, on the other hand, was too captivated at the sight of Katerina's boobs to be able to say anything.

'And you will come to my party, too?' asked the bride-to-be.

My mum's eyes lit up.

'Oh, no,' I jumped in. 'They already have plans. And anyway, an occasion like tonight is more for family and friends, isn't it? You don't want a bunch of strangers there getting in the way.'

As soon as the words were out, I realised how harsh they must've sounded and I felt terrible. More so when I realised Mum's disappointment. But I had to say something, didn't I? And I was thinking on my feet. Not that that stopped me from feeling a complete bitch.

Even Katerina appeared saddened, but at least she quickly recovered, hastily saying something to her parents as she picked up her loaded shopping bags. 'We have to go now,' she said, returning her attention back to my family and me. 'We have so much to do.'

She, Efthimeos and Maria bid their goodbyes and headed out to the kitchen, the two females in the trio excitedly chattering as they went.

Thank goodness! Wedding danger averted!

'You're here for Lydia's birthday, I take it,' said Yiannis.

Bugger! Unlike Tammy, I'd forgotten about him.

'We most certainly are,' replied Mum. 'We're a very close family too, you know.'

'So why didn't you come to last night's celebrations?' Yiannis asked. He turned to me, confused. 'Lydia, why didn't you call your family and tell them to come down?'

I'd been so wrapped up in preventing the Livingstons from finding out about my supposed role in Katerina's wedding, I'd totally forgotten about that side of things. And as a result, I honestly didn't know what to say.

'The birthday that isn't supposed to be happening, you mean?' said Mum. She maintained a graceful smile—one that involved her lips, just not the rest of her face.

'Well, it wasn't really a party,' I said, speaking way too quickly. 'And I didn't know anything about it beforehand, did I, Sam?' I turned to my unlikely ally, in desperate need of someone to back me up.

'No, she didn't, Mrs Livingston,' he said, taking my cue. 'It was something I arranged, just a quiet affair with a cake Maria kindly made and a few candles, nothing too exciting.'

'Oh, come on,' said Yiannis. 'It was more than that. Sam, you of all people know we don't do quiet around these parts.'

Despite her best efforts, Mum struggled to maintain her smile. 'A cake, you say? How very kind of your mother to do that. Of course, baking a cake is something I'd normally do, but Lydia did insist she wanted nothing of the sort this year.' The hurt was written all over her face.

'I think I'll go and seek out Luke and Johnny,' said Pete, tentatively getting up from his seat, 'to make sure they're all right.'

He reminded me of a rat leaving a sinking ship.

'All I can say is that it's good you two didn't have far to walk home,' continued Yiannis, completely oblivious to the growing tension around the table. 'Not after the amount of alcohol that you drank.'

I willed him to please shut up but it was too late. The damage had already been done.

In a surprise move Mum got to her feet and picked up her bag.

'Where are you going?' I asked. We couldn't just end it there, she had to understand. 'You're not leaving, are you?'

'Yes, Lydia. I am. It's obvious you have better things to do with your new-found friends here,' she said. 'And who am I to get in your way.'

Again, I looked to Sam for some assistance.

'Please, Mrs Livingston. Stay. Let me get you a drink,' he said, his attempts at appeasement as much use as mine.

'That's very kind of you,' Mum replied, 'but not necessary.'

Dad shook his head at me as he also rose to his feet. 'Come on, Tammy,' he instructed.

My stomach sank.

'Mum, Dad, please!' I called out. 'I didn't know anything about it.'

My words were to no avail and I was forced to watch them go.

CHAPTER FOURTEEN

The crow does not take the eye out of another crow.

I decided not to go to Katerina's engagement party that night; after what had happened, it wouldn't have been right. But neither did I go to see my parents. I couldn't front the hurt on Mum's face; seeing it and the disappointment on Dad's the first time had been enough. And I certainly wasn't in the mood to put up with Pete's gloating; having always got a kick out of me being in trouble, I knew he wouldn't be able to help himself.

Instead, I simply stayed away from everyone. I kept to myself, again wondering how one little white lie could lead to all of this. All the while I was hoping that in the meantime Mum and Dad would come searching me out, which by now they evidently weren't going to do. Then again, why would they? I was the one in the wrong, after all. In fact, the only person who called on me was Sam and I definitely didn't want to talk to him. The last thing I needed at the moment was a lecture on doing the right thing—as if I didn't already know that.

Of course, I didn't blame him for his insistence. Time was moving on and I still hadn't confessed to the Fatolitis that I wasn't really in a position to do their catering, let alone the reasons why. And I couldn't do that until I'd admitted my deceit to the Livingstons, something I knew I'd put off for long enough.

I knocked on Mum and Dad's hotel room door, my heart pumping as I steadied myself, ready to tell them the truth. It took ages before Luke and Johnny answered, the pair of them snorkelled up as if about to hit the water.

'Grandma! Grandma!' they shouted. 'Aunty Lydia's here.'

They stared at me through their goggles as if I was some sort of alien species not to be trusted.

'You're in trouble,' they said, almost revelling in my misfortune.

'You don't know the half of it,' I replied.

Just then, Mum came up behind them. 'I wondered how long it would take you,' she said. 'Waiting for us to come to you, were you?'

She always did know me a bit too well.

'Not at all,' I lied. 'I just thought I'd give you a bit of time to yourself, that's all.'

I could see she didn't believe me.

'Well, don't just stand there,' she said. 'Come in, come in.'

'Ah, the prodigal daughter returns,' said my darling brother, right on cue.

On this occasion, however, I knew what was good for me and resisted the urge to bite back. After all, I was in enough trouble as it was.

'Now don't be rude to your sister, Pete,' said Dad, although I suspected his words were more for Mum's benefit than mine. She always did hate it when we squabbled.

'Thanks, Dad,' I said, regardless, his ensuing flash of hostility only confirming my fears.

Tammy appeared from what I assumed to be the bathroom and I did a double take. She looked different somehow, more grown-up, and I felt sure she didn't usually wear make-up. Then again, I was more used to seeing her head-down, preoccupied with this text and that text on her mobile as opposed to having her look me directly in the eye. Her phone, bizarrely enough, was now nowhere in sight.

'Hiya, Aunty Lydia,' she said, friendly as anything. Her words stirred up even more curiosity considering that up until now I hadn't realised the girl could talk.

Still, it was nice to hear at least one amicable voice in the group and it spurred me on to say what I'd actually come to say.

'I'm here to apologise,' I ventured, hoping to sound more positive about it than I truly felt. 'For the other day.'

'And so you should,' said Mum, quick as anything and going from her tone, clearly in no frame of mind to make it easy for me.

'I agree,' said Dad.

'All that rubbish about your birthday being a non-event this year,' Mum carried on. 'The only reason we came here, Lydia, was so you didn't have to spend it on your own. There we were, imagining you having a right old miserable time... and yet there you are eating cake and goodness knows what else with some other family and all behind our backs. You must think we're fools!'

'Mum, I didn't know they were gonna make that cake. I didn't know about the party full stop.'

'Anyone would think you're ashamed of us!'

I began to feel desperate.

'Of course I'm not ashamed of you, Mum. I'm not ashamed of any of you. How could you even think that? It's just...' I trailed off, not knowing how to explain best.

Mum rounded on me, not quite ready to listen yet anyway.

'It's just what, Lydia? Even when we were invited to that girl's engagement do, you couldn't make our excuses quick enough. So, what're we supposed to think? I know Luke and Johnny can be a bit of a handful at times and Lord knows your brother can be a pain when he wants to be, but...'

'Cheers, Mum!' said Pete, not that she heard.

'But the way you've treated us is inexcusable, young lady. And what makes you think we deserve that I just don't know.'

'I don't think anything of the sort, Mum. What happened the other day wasn't about any of you lot, it was about me. And when I explain, I know the two of you, Mum and Dad, are gonna be even more disappointed and you, Pete, are gonna laugh at me until the day I die, but,' I plonked myself down on the sofa, almost too embarrassed to continue, 'I think I need to start from the beginning.'

Mum and Dad shared a look of concern and they too, took a seat.

'Go on,' said Mum. 'We're listening.'

They allowed me a moment to gather my thoughts.

'So, you know how I've always had this thing about finding Mr Right?' I began.

'Yes,' said Mum.

'And you're all aware of the work I've put into me to make sure I'm Mrs Right?'

'Yes, of course we are.'

'But do you understand *why* I've done what I've done?' I asked. 'I mean *really* understand?'

Mum, Dad and Pete just stared at me blankly.

'Well, if I'm being honest,' Mum eventually replied, 'no.'

'I don't see what this has to do with the last few days,' added Dad.

'So, if you lot don't understand, even though I've explained it enough times, how is anyone else expected to get their head around it?'

'Well they won't, will they?' said Pete. 'Because it's a crackpot way of thinking to begin with.'

'Exactly,' I said.

'I get it,' said Tammy, much to everyone's surprise, not least mine. 'We're doing this thing at school in our history class. About the changing roles of women and the different expectations placed on them today compared to what they used to be.'

'Wow,' I replied. 'We didn't do anything like that when I was there.'

'And I agree with you, Aunty Lydia,' she carried on, confident as anything. 'All that nineties stuff about women being able to have it all and do everything, well it was all right in theory, but in practice it turned out to be like everything else. It didn't work, did it? Not for most people anyway, not for normal people like us. We'd have to get rid of the granddads and Uncle Pete's of this world for that to happen.'

To say I felt gobsmacked would be an understatement. Tammy hadn't just managed to string more than a couple of sentences together; her sentences had actually made sense; the girl had way more intelligence than I'd ever had the decency to credit her with.

Of course, I wasn't the only one who was momentarily speechless, but I was sure given time Dad and Pete would get over it.

'Thank you,' I said, genuinely grateful and touched by the support my niece had just shown me.

'You're welcome,' she replied, like it was nothing.

'I still don't see what this has to do with anything,' said Mum, dragging us all back to the matter at hand.

'No, me neither,' said Dad.

'But that's my point. If you lot can't appreciate where it is I'm coming from, Tammy excluded from all this, of course... How will anyone else? Which brings me to when I met Sam... and explains why I told him I was a chef.'

'Sorry?' said Mum. 'What was that last bit again?'

'I told him I was a chef. With my own restaurant back in England, and that I was here to research Greek cooking.'

There, I'd said it. My secret was out.

'Ha!' said Pete.

'But why, Lydia?' asked Mum, not just aghast, but obviously recalling how disastrous I actually am in a kitchen. 'Why would you tell anyone that?'

'Because I didn't want people to think I was the loser you all think I am.'

'If the cap fits!' said Pete.

'Then the Fatolitis found out I was a chef.'

Again, my brother couldn't help himself. 'Which you're not,' he added, at the same time starting to titter.

'So, they started making me all these gorgeous meals that were meant to help me with my supposed research and you know what I'm like when it comes to food.'

'Oh, do we.' He put his hand in his mouth to try and prevent all-out laughter.

'So, I just played along. But somehow Sam ended up finding out the truth and used it to blackmail me into going out with him.'

'Fantastic!'

'And things went from bad to worse.'

'He blackmailed you?' asked Dad. 'And I thought he seemed an all right chap.'

Unable to quite contain himself, Pete began to really lose control. 'You couldn't write it, could you?' he said, clutching his stomach.

'So, he's not really your boyfriend, then?' asked Mum.

'No, Mum, he's not.'

'But the two of you would like to be in a relationship, wouldn't you?'

I ignored her question in much the same way I'd been trying to ignore Pete.

'It gets worse,' I added.

'Worse,' said Mum.

'How can it get any worse?' struggled Pete.

'Well, I inadvertently mentioned my birthday to Sam and he told Maria, which is why she made the cake I knew nothing about beforehand, by the way.' I felt the need to clarify that. 'Then Katerina's wedding caterers let her down and obviously because the Fatolitis thought I was this famous chef from England—'

'No,' said Mum, anticipating what came next.

By now Pete was rolling on the floor.

'Yes,' I replied. 'They asked if I'd step in and do the honours.'

'But you didn't say yes, did you?' asked Mum.

Not for the first time, my silence said it all.

Pete was in absolute hysterics at this point and I noticed a slight titter escape Tammy's mouth as well.

Mum and Dad, however, appeared mortified.

'What else could I say?' I asked. 'Things had already gone too far for me to say anything else!'

'But, Lydia, you can't cook,' said Mum to the sound of Pete's laughing frenzy. 'How on earth did you think you were going to get away with it?'

'That's the problem. I didn't think, did I? Which is why I'm in this mess to start with. I'm in trouble with you... with them... even Sam thinks I'm out of order and he's a bleeding blackmailer.'

Upon hearing this, Pete let out another loud howl. 'Stop, please,' he called out, 'I think I'm gonna pee my pants.'

I hoped he would.

'Anyway, now you know the reasons why I didn't invite you to my place and why I didn't want you talking to the Fatolitis,' I finished.

I waited for my parents to say something, hoping they'd tell me I'd worried long enough and that everything would be all right. After all, isn't that what parents are supposed to do when it comes to their children?

Apparently not.

At least not in my case. Rather, mine just sat there staring at me all agog, as if I was from another planet.

CHAPTER FIFTEEN

The misfortunes of the first ones, a bridge for the second ones.

Now that I'd stopped burying my head in the sand, it was time to face the Fatolitis. They were going to hate me for what I was about to do, I knew that. And them being a passionate lot, I fully anticipated the fallout that was, no doubt, to follow. I didn't relish the prospect.

On my way back from Mum and Dad's hotel, I imagined the pure disdain in Yiannis's eyes and heard the string of fork-tongued expletives spitting out from the usually jovial Efthimeos. Poor Maria would feel used and foolish for trying to help me with a non-existent culinary quest—all the while trying to comfort her now inconsolable daughter. The very same daughter who'd have no qualms in going back to the traditional plate throwing, taking it to a whole new level with me as her intended target. Then they'd probably chuck both me and my belongings out onto the street, leaving me no choice but to leave the island altogether. And as if that wouldn't be bad enough, this being such a small island with quite a close-knit community, the odds were I'd have to swim for it, on account of the captain of the boat to Kos refusing me safe passage.

I sat down on one of the roadside benches telling myself I couldn't blame them. This situation was, after all, of my own making. Not that that made my owning up any easier and, although I tried to plan what I was going to say, words quickly failed me. How do you tell someone you're about to ruin the biggest day of their life?

A scooter pulled up next to me and I glanced up to see Sam disembarking. Just what I didn't need right now.

'I've been looking for you,' he said.

'I know,' I replied. 'I just needed a bit of time.'

He plonked himself down on the seat next to me.

'I'm on my way to tell them now,' I said, kicking at the dust by my feet. 'That's if I can figure out how best to say things.'

'Would it help if I came with you?' he asked.

His offer of support sounded genuine enough. But then again, hadn't that been the case when he'd offered to help me get rid of Mum and Dad the other day? Furthermore, as I considered his relationship with the Fatolitis, I realised his might not be the fairest of shoulders to lean on. However, that didn't stop a part of me thinking that having Sam at my side was better than having no one.

'What? So, they can hate us both instead of just me?' I eventually said. 'What would be the point in that?'

He took my hand and looked me straight in the eye. 'Like you've already said, we're in this together.'

The nervous butterflies already fluttering in my stomach suddenly began to run amok and I took a deep breath in an attempt to calm them down.

'Together,' I replied, grateful.

We got to our feet and with our hands still firmly clasped, Sam indicated to his scooter. 'Shall we?'

'I'd rather walk,' I said, wanting to delay the inevitable for as long as possible.

'No problem,' he simply replied and still not letting go of each other, we set off to face the music.

'Lydia! Sam!' Katerina called out, as we made our approach.

I watched her excitedly hail our arrival to the rest of the family, who immediately came running in response; their collective relief was almost as tangible as the out-and-out dread that Sam and I were experiencing. Although as they all took a turn at throwing their arms around us, I could feel my heart sinking that bit further with each and every well-intentioned hug. In fact, in those few moments it took all my inner strength not to turn on my heels and flee.

'Didn't I say Lydia wouldn't let us down,' said Efthimeos. He looked to his wife and daughter at the same time as I looked to Sam. 'You women, you worry about nothing.'

Maria signalled for us both to come and sit, obviously as eager as her daughter to get the wedding reception organised once and for all. Then without even waiting for us to do as we were told she was back off into the kitchen again, no doubt carrying out her role as hostess, putting together some serious refreshments.

I remained standing.

'Where have you been?' asked Katerina. 'We have so much to talk about, things to discuss!'

'That's why I'm here,' I replied. 'There's something I need to—'

Maria reappeared with a tray of biscuits, cake and glasses of orange juice and I found myself faltering, still not quite sure how to put things. Moreover, as I looked to my hosts, desperately not wanting to continue, I could see the seriousness in my face suddenly reflected in theirs.

A nod from Sam, however, and I felt encouraged to go on, telling myself I just needed to get this over and done with.

'It's about the wedding,' I began.

'Yoohoo!' a female voice suddenly called out from behind.

I immediately recognised who it belonged to and, falling silent, I turned to spot Mum rushing towards me, Tammy in tow.

'What're you two doing here?' I asked, wondering what all the haste was about. Only thirty minutes or so ago, Mum had been so speechless she hadn't been able to move, let alone run.

'I'm not too late, am I?' she asked.

'For what?' I replied.

Mum leaned into me. 'Surely you didn't think I'd let you down, did you?' She turned to everyone else. 'With a wedding reception to organise and very little time in which to do it, I thought I'd come and offer my services, if that's all right with you?'

Yiannis did the honours and translated to the rest of the Fatolitis.

'Yes, yes,' said Efthimeos, very much to his family's agreement.

She gave Sam and me a sly wink, willing us to play along.

'Now, tell me to go away if you want, Lydia,' she continued. 'You're the expert. I just thought with you doing the cooking, who's going to concentrate on all the other stuff that'll need doing?'

Inside, I began to freak. What other stuff? There isn't going to be a wedding reception. At least not one I'm involved in!

'Which is where we come in,' said Tammy, obviously in on the act.

My niece may have been talking to me, but her smile was fixed on Yiannis, the reason behind the make-up and discarded mobile phone suddenly all too clear.

Fantastic! A love-struck teenager on top of everything else.

'And you already know from your restaurant, Lydia, how difficult these events can be sometimes,' Mum said. She pointedly turned her attention to the bride-to-be. 'Things can so easily go wrong if you're not careful.'

'She's right,' said Katerina, panicking at the mere thought. Understandably, the last thing she wanted was anything else going awry, a state of mind I could see my Mum was counting on. 'We need more help.'

'So now we've got that sorted,' said Mum, coming across all efficient. 'Let's get down to business.' Now really taking charge of the situation, she pulled a pen and notebook out of her bag, ready to hold court. 'Come on, everyone. Gather around.'

'First thing's first,' said Efthimeos, as if suddenly remembering his manners. 'What would you like to drink?'

'Ooh, a cup of tea would be very nice,' said Mum. Efthimeos gestured to Maria that she stay exactly where she was and that he would make it; the rest of us did as we were told and took our seats accordingly.

Of course, Sam and I were more reluctant about doing so than the others, wondering what my mother thought she was playing at. Although much to our continued dismay, any such concerns counted for nothing and she instead directed her attention to the remaining Fatolitis.

'Right,' she said, 'I take it Lydia has already mentioned the rustic nature of her cuisine?'

Excuse me.

Not that she gave them time to answer.

'So, I was thinking food-wise you might want to stick with the chef's signature dishes? Especially considering we don't have much time to play with.'

What chef? What signature dishes?

'Definitely,' replied an emphatic Katerina—thanks to Mum's earlier warning, the poor girl was justifiably still preoccupied with what could go wrong.

'So, there's vegetable soup to start,' said Mum, noting it down, 'followed by roast beef and Yorkshire pudding for the main.'

I couldn't believe what I was hearing. We're not talking about Sunday lunch around at yours here, Mum, we're talking about someone's wedding.

She looked up with a smile. 'And how does cheesecake for dessert sound?'

Oh... my... goodness...

'Yummy,' said Sam, much to my horror getting into the swing of things. At the same time, the Fatolitis nodded their approval, although in their case I couldn't help but think that in spite of their conviction, they didn't have a clue what they were agreeing to.

'And how many guests are we catering for?' Mum asked, just as Efthimeos reappeared, cup of tea in hand. 'Thank you,' she said, like butter wouldn't melt.

'Fifty,' replied Katerina.

Dear God, please take me now.

Unlike me, upon hearing this my mother didn't even flinch, and if she saw my anxiety level rising, she certainly didn't acknowledge it. Instead, she put the pen to her lips and began glancing about the bar like a true professional, ready to move the discussion forward.

'She's good, isn't she?' said Sam, discreetly leaning my way.

'I can't believe you're falling for this,' I replied and, getting more and more worried by the second, I looked to the Fatolitis who continued to hang on her every word. 'I can't believe anyone's falling for this.'

'Of course, we can use the tables and chairs you already have, a bit of titivating and no one will be any the wiser,' said Mum— now the consummate interior designer on top of everything else. 'But what about the colour scheme? Did you have anything in mind?'

Katerina turned to Maria and a Greek consultation followed. 'We were thinking something bright, like red or that really dazzling pink,' she eventually replied.

'Good choice,' said Mum, again jotting down a few notes.

'No expense spared,' added Efthimeos, as if feeling the need to clarify.

'Naturally,' replied Mum. 'We all want what's best when it comes to our daughters, now, don't we?'

Convinced there was a message in there for me somewhere, under the circumstances I was damned if I knew what it was. Yes, I might have started this charade, but I certainly couldn't see how her carrying it on was in my best interests. Especially when feeding fifty Greeks roast beef and Yorkshire pudding was the best she could come up with.

'Well, Mr and Mrs Fatolitis,' said Mum. 'and the lovely Katerina, of course, I think we have all we need for now.'

They all smiled, satisfied everything was finally sorted once and for all.

'Although I'm sorry to have to say this,' Mum then continued, 'but I can see from here that the kitchen you have is way too small for what we need.' I almost choked at this statement.

What? Where else do you suppose you're going to do all this blooming cooking then? And why go through all this rigmarole if at the end of it you're just gonna say we can't do it?

I could see I wasn't the only one worried by Mum's words; the Fatolitis suddenly appeared equally fretted.

'Wouldn't you agree, Lydia?' she added.

Oh, so now you want to include me?

I made a show of glancing over. 'Oh yes, way too small to prepare for a wedding reception,' I replied, maintaining the view that a small kitchen was way better than no kitchen at all.

'Which leads me to wonder where we're going to get everything done,' said Mum, turning the floor over to the rest of us. 'Ideas, anyone?'

CHAPTER SIXTEEN

Whoever has the beard has the combs.

If it had been up to me we, would have made the trip to our destination on foot. But whereas I'd had no choice but to get used to the trek up and along the top road, Mum, Dad and Pete had taken one look at the hill in front of them and said 'no chance'.

Naturally, this meant taking two taxis: me, Pete and Tammy in one, with my parents and the twins in the other. Although as our journey drew to a close, I wondered why we were even bothering; so what if this place had everything the supremo wedding caterer could possibly need? We still wouldn't be able to pull off the job and instead of just me looking foolish as a result, now we all would.

Then again, as we disembarked our vehicles, I had to admit that as a family we did look pretty mad as hatters to begin with. We'd always been something of a motley crew and today was no different.

Pete let out a prolonged, drawn-out whistle, surprise, surprise, leaving me to pay the driver as he took in the building before us. 'Nice pad,' he said.

'Yes, well, you just remember you're here to keep an eye on Luke and Johnny,' I reminded him. 'Which means if anything gets broken or goes missing, it's on your head.'

'So, what's my job, then?' asked Tammy.

I looked over at Mum clutching her trusty shopping bag and its secrets as she and Dad tried to round up my nephews. 'No doubt we'll find out,' I said.

We left them to catch up and as the three of us set off up the drive, I spotted Sam already at the door waiting to greet us.

'Welcome to my humble abode,' he said, gesturing us in.

'Nothing humble about it, mate,' said Pete, and as we stepped over the threshold, I found myself forced to agree with him for a change.

One big, open plan space, it looked like one of those interiors featured in a glossy magazine. Blinding white walls adorned with gorgeously bright artwork; big inviting sofas—all cream, of course, placed to give the ultra-modern fireplace centre stage; and the most beautiful glass dining table that could easily have seated ten—nothing at all like the pokey little wooden number we all had to squeeze around every Sunday. Then there was the kitchen beyond, all stainless steel and with just the right amount of granite. The house really was to die for.

I followed Pete over to the giant picture windows, taking in a view far better than the one I'd imagined it to have during the bus ride from Pothia that day. I knew it'd be fantastic, I just hadn't realised how fantastic.

'You've certainly landed on your feet here, sis,' he said, captivated.

'Firstly,' I replied, 'my feet haven't landed anywhere. And secondly, Sam's only the caretaker.' I turned to look at him. 'Aren't you, Sam?'

He appeared almost embarrassed at me having clarified this, not that him being the hired help seemed to bother my brother in any way.

'Nice work if you can get it,' he said.

Luke and Johnny suddenly burst in from outside, immediately wide-eyed at the sight that met them. 'Wow!' they called out, eager to touch anything and everything they could get their hands on.

'This is so not a good idea,' I said, chasing after them to retrieve and put back everything they went to pick up.

'Can we come in?' said Mum. 'Very nice,' she added, glancing about the place.

'You've done well for yourself here, love,' said Dad.

Sam smiled my way, not even attempting to contradict them. But unlike him, I most certainly couldn't see the funny side; however, having stressed the fact enough times already that the two of us were in no way romantically involved and nor would we ever be, I didn't see much point in going through it all again.

'So, Mrs Livingston,' said Sam. 'Will it do the job?'

Much to my mortification, as Luke and Johnny began bouncing about on the giant sofas, Mum was already opening one kitchen cupboard door after another, trying to suss out where everything was. The responsibility for this event was obviously going to her head to the point that she'd lost all sense of boundaries. 'More than comfortably,' she replied, satisfied with her assessment, 'and like I've said, please call me Margot.'

'I must say, it's good of your employers to let us do this,' said Dad. Although if they could see how much their house was being ransacked at the moment, I very much doubted they'd have agreed to anything.

'They're good people,' replied Sam. 'They even wished they could've been here to help out.'

Now *that* I couldn't believe.

'Shall we get started, then?' suggested Mum, making a beeline for the dining table.

Apart from Luke and Johnny, we all followed suit and took a seat.

'Now I took the liberty of jotting a few things down,' she said, once again producing her notebook and pen. 'To make sure I didn't forget anything.'

'A few,' I replied, staring at the pages and pages of copious scribbling.

'Organisation is key when it comes to events like this, Lydia,' she said, starting to flick through them.

'Something I thought you'd know,' jumped in Pete, 'being the chef at a fancy restaurant and all that.'

I poked my tongue out at him by way of a response. Although at the same time, I knew my brother did have a point

'Now, as I'll be doing the actual catering,' Mum continued, 'it makes sense for me and your dad to do the food shop. That way, there's less margin for error. And I was thinking you, Lydia, could sort out all the decorations and flowers etcetera. You might not be able to cook, but you certainly know your stuff in that department.'

The boys continued to have fun on the sofa.

'Okay,' I said, 'I'm happy with that.'

'Although I do think you should take Sam with you so he can keep an eye on your spending,' she added, 'because we all know how good you can be at that as well.'

Pete sniggered and Sam's eyes lit up.

Great, I thought. A few more hours with him was all I needed.

'And before you go complaining,' Mum was clearly on a roll, 'I know Mr Fatolitis said money was no object, but that doesn't mean we have to take him at his word, does it?'

'But—' I turned to Luke and Johnny, their excitement at being in a new place getting a bit too loud for me to be heard properly. 'Come on, boys,' I said. 'We're trying to discuss important stuff here.'

They stopped what they were doing, coming over all angelic as they looked back at me.

'Thank you,' I said, able to return my attention to the adults in the room once more.

'What I was going to say,' I explained, 'is where on earth are we supposed to do all of this non-spending? From what I've seen of Kalymnos, I think we might struggle.'

Suddenly, there was an almighty crash from the other side of the room.

'What was that?' I asked, leaping out of my seat to investigate.

'Sam, I'm so sorry,' I said, spotting my nephews hovering over what was once a beautiful vase, now lying on the floor in pieces.

'We didn't mean to,' said Luke.

'We were only looking at it,' said Johnny.

'And it just fell,' they both said.

'That's why you look with your eyes, not your hands,' I scolded, kneeling down in an attempt to pick up the pieces.

Sam appeared at my side with a dustpan and brush. 'Don't worry about it,' he said, calm as anything. 'I'm sure no one will miss it.' He gently took the ceramic shards from my hands and began clearing up the rest of the mess.

'But it looks expensive,' I said.

'It was an accident,' wailed the twins.

'Whatever it cost,' Dad called out, 'Lydia will cover it.'

'What?' I asked, shocked at the mere suggestion. There was no way I could afford it.

'Well, you are the reason we're all here,' said Pete.

'Your brother's right,' agreed Mum.

I couldn't believe the injustice of their words.

'But these two are the ones who broke it,' I argued.

As the three of them stared at me like judges and jury, it was apparent my protests were futile. Still, at least Tammy had the decency to remain quiet.

'Honestly, it's only a vase,' said Sam, 'it doesn't matter.'

Luke and Johnny began scrutinizing first Sam and then me.

'Are you Aunty Lydia's boyfriend?' asked one.

'Everyone says you are,' said the other.

'Christ have mercy!' I replied. 'What's wrong with everyone around here? No, he is not!'

Sam leaned into them both, his whispering causing the two of them to giggle.

'What?' I asked. 'What did you just say?'

I watched him head off with the evidence, ignoring me, and I glared at the twins as they too refused to answer my question. 'Don't touch anything else,' I said, finally returning to my seat at the table.

'We could always go over to Kos,' said Sam, from over by the bin, 'for the decorations. It's a bigger island so should give us more of a choice. We could even make a day of it?'

'Oh, aye,' said Pete.

'Oh, aye, nothing,' I replied, still reeling over the twins.

'The lady doth protest too much,' said Pete. The man really didn't know when to shut up.

'That's exactly what I was thinking,' said Sam, although who gave him permission to join in goodness only knew.

'If we can just get back to the matter at hand,' I said, refusing to be drawn into their childishness.

'Thank you, Lydia,' said Mum.

Like I was moving things on for *her* benefit.

'Now, obviously because it's an evening wedding,' she continued, 'we can do a lot of the preparations the night before.'

An evening wedding. I sighed at the romantic nature of it all, for the first time recognising this event was going to be harder to get through in more ways than just the catering. *And here I am stuck on the side-lines.* Something apparently no one else had considered, the heartless so and so's, despite them all knowing it should've been my reception we were discussing not someone else's.

'Which gives us most of the day to get the cooking done. We'll have to do all of that here, of course,' she said, 'and then ferry it down to the bar while the ceremony's taking place.'

'But how do we keep everything warm?' asked Tammy.

'Good question,' replied Mum.

By now, they were all really getting into the swing of things. But the more organised they became, the more unfeeling they appeared with regard to my still unmarried position in all of this, and I felt myself retreating into a childlike sulk because of it.

'We can always ask a couple of nearby restaurants if they can lend us their microwaves?' said Sam. 'Not ideal, but under the circumstances I don't suppose we have much choice.'

'Aren't you the one with all the answers,' I replied.

Mum flashed me a look designed to put me in my place and, under normal circumstances, it probably would've worked. On this occasion, however, I refused to let it. After all, she of all people should've understood how difficult this would be and I begrudged the fact that she clearly didn't.

'You know,' said Dad, 'I think we just might get away with this.'

I almost laughed. 'What's this we business? That's the first contribution you've made.'

I knew I was being juvenile and self-indulgent, ungrateful even, especially considering they were all only trying to save me from the biggest embarrassment of my life so far. But I couldn't help it and it didn't matter anyway. Once again, anything I had to say was completely ignored; Mum preferred to consult her notes rather than acknowledge any distress her daughter might be experiencing.

'When it comes to the actual reception,' she said, 'Tammy, Sam and Dad, you'll be doing the waiting on. And Lydia, you'll be helping me in the kitchen.'

Everyone else grinned, looking forward to their involvement.

'What about me?' said Pete, obviously feeling a tad left out.

'What about you?' I asked.

Mum moved swiftly on.

'It'll be your job to look after the twins,' she explained. 'The last thing we'll need is any disruption from those two. Speaking of whom,' she began looking around, all of us suddenly realising how quiet the room was, 'where are Luke and Johnny?'

CHAPTER SEVENTEEN

The one hand washes the other and both wash the face.

S am and I raced down onto the roadside in front of the house. With only one long stretch of road and no turn offs, the twins could only have gone left or right and we both felt safe in the knowledge that locating them would be easy enough.

'Luke! Johnny!' Sam called out, setting off in one direction.

'Johnny! Luke!' I called out, setting off in the other.

I looked ahead into the distance, but there was no sign of them. I checked the bushes as I went just to make sure; neither was there any sound to indicate they might be hiding somewhere. Obviously, children didn't just vanish and I told myself they must have gone the other way. However, as I turned around, I spotted Sam making his return and realised I was wrong. Just like me, he appeared empty-handed.

'Where can they be?' I asked. I didn't know whether to be angry or worried about the little blighters.

'They can only have gone up the back,' said Sam, 'because they're definitely not down here.'

I stared up at the unforgiving mountainside and began to freak a little. 'You mean up there?'

Dry and arid with lots of caves and crags to explore, it was just the playground for two hyperactive little boys, and I should've known the two of them wouldn't be able to resist. Nevertheless, a rock face coupled with my nephews wasn't exactly the best of combinations. In fact, it was more like an accident waiting to happen.

'Shit!' I said.

'I'll get help,' said Sam.

We ran back up the drive and into the house, where he immediately got on the phone.

'We can't find them anywhere,' said Mum. 'We've searched the whole house and they're not here.'

'We think they've headed up into the mountains,' I explained, doing my best not to panic. 'But don't worry. Sam's going to find them.' At least I hoped he was going to find them.

Tammy rushed in from the rear garden. 'The gate up the top's open,' she said, confirming our fears. 'Uncle Pete's gone for a scout around the rocks.'

We all held our breath waiting for Sam to finish on the phone.

'Help's on its way,' he said, finally putting the receiver down. 'I'll just get some stuff together.' He hastily left the room, quickly returning with huge, coiled-up stretches of rope and a heavy-duty rucksack—a sight that seemed to underline the seriousness of the situation.

'Oh my word,' said Mum, anxiety written all over her face.

'These are just in case,' he said, pausing to reassure her. 'I'm sure we won't need them.'

'Of course you won't,' said Dad, placing a comforting hand on Mum's back. Although I could see he was putting a brave face on it for both their sakes.

'You're right, Dad,' I reiterated. 'They can't have gone anywhere near far enough for all that malarkey. Not in this short time.' But just like him, I was also trying to convince myself as much as I was anyone else.

It didn't take long before car horns began beeping outside and a stream of other climbers began letting themselves in, with Sam immediately organising them into a coordinated search party. In the meantime, all the rest of us could do was watch, listen and feel grateful for such expert help. I realised I'd never been so relieved to see so much Lycra in all my life.

The group started making for the door, while Sam hastily grabbed a pen and scribbled something down on a piece of paper.

'Here's my mobile number,' he said, handing it to me. 'Just in case they turn up back here.' He made a point of approaching Mum. 'Try not to worry, Mrs Livingston,' he said, 'if they're up there somewhere, we'll have them down again safe and sound before you know it.'

Mum smiled, clearly appreciating his words. 'Thank you,' she said.

We stood watching as they left, feeling powerless.

'Tammy,' I said, 'do you fancy finding your way around the kitchen and making us all a nice cup of tea?' Drinking tea is what you do in times of trouble, isn't it?

'Sure,' she replied, seemingly glad to be doing something useful.

'I'll never forgive myself if something happens to them!' said Mum. She plonked herself down at the dining table. 'And what do we tell Steve and Jill?'

'No point thinking like that, love,' said Dad. 'Like Sam says, he'll have those twins back here soon enough.'

'Yes, well, when he does, I'll bloody well chuck them off that mountain myself,' said Mum, her fear speaking more than anything.

I went up behind her and gave her a hug. 'No, you won't. You'll throw your arms around the pair of them and tell them how much you love them.'

She let out a little smile. 'I will, won't I?' she said. 'And while I'm at it I'll wring their bloody necks. Putting us through all this!'

Tammy came back with a tray and we all took a cup.

'It's my fault though,' I said. 'If I hadn't shouted at them like I did, they'd probably still be here. In fact, if it weren't for me, they'd be in the UK right now—like all of us would. Me and my bright ideas.'

I felt terrible. Everyone present was on this island in this house because of me, and as if that wasn't enough, trying to clean up the mess after me. Yet, in spite of all this, I'd still spent the last hour with my lip out because they didn't feel sorry for me. Talk about being selfish.

'I'm sorry about earlier,' I said. 'For acting like a spoiled brat. It just hurts being involved in someone else's wedding, you know? Anyway, the twins disappearing like this has certainly put things into perspective, so from now on, there'll be no more sulking.'

'And there'll be no more swanning off to distant shores either,' said Mum. 'Not if things like this are going to happen.'

'Well, I'm glad we're here,' said Tammy. 'And as for you being to blame, Aunty Lydia, we all know what Luke and Johnny are like.'

'Tammy!' scolded Mum. She would never have anyone say anything bad about her grandchildren.

'What?' Tammy replied. 'It's true. If they hadn't disappeared now, it'd be somewhere else at some other time. Causing trouble is what they do best.'

Considering what was happening, I found her honesty quite brave and I wondered if all sisters took this kind of view when it came to their siblings. I know I certainly did about Pete and could be equally blunt with it.

Mum smiled. 'They are independent little boys, aren't they?'

Dad gave a little chuckle. 'That's one way of putting it.'

'Trouble is, they don't have any fear either,' said Mum, her worry starting to show again. 'And they could end up in all sorts of bother because of it.'

'They'll be fine,' said Tammy. 'You'll see. Like the time they managed to lock themselves in that container for hours. They were rescued then and they'll be rescued now.'

She was right; the little buggers did seem to have nine lives. They were always getting themselves into one scrape or another and coming out the other side relatively unscathed.

We fell into a silence and I could see it wasn't just me hoping that would be the case on this occasion too. But we all knew Luke and Johnny's nine lives had quickly become eight, then seven, then six and so on. In fact, everyone who'd ever met them had lost count of exactly how many they had left.

I began to imagine the two of them huddling together on some precipice, rocks crumbling at their feet, stones falling away at the slightest of movements. Of course, they wouldn't have thought to take water with them either and out in such high temperatures I knew they must be getting dehydrated by now—even more so if they hadn't managed to find some shade and were out in the searing sunshine.

Sitting there for what felt like way too long already, the thought-fuelled silence finally became too much.

'I can't just sit here,' I said at last, getting up from my seat. 'I've got to do something. Maybe I should go and have another look around.'

'I'll come with you,' said Tammy, clearly feeling the same way.

We'd just got to the door when we heard voices.

'Oh, thank goodness,' I said, recognising my nephews' inimitable chatter.

'Grandma! Grandma!' chorused Luke and Johnny, bursting into the room. 'We got all the way up there!' They pointed in the general direction of the mountainside, completely oblivious to all the fuss they'd caused.

'Oh, come here, you two,' said Mum, jumping up and scooping them into her arms to squeeze the life out of them. 'Thank God you're okay.'

'They especially liked the bit where they were lowered down on the ropes,' said Pete, eyes widened and brows raised to emphasize just how dangerous their position had been. 'Who knows what would've happened if this chap hadn't come along when he did, eh, kids?' He turned to Sam. 'Cheers, mate.'

'Yes, we got to wear helmets,' said Luke.

'And these harness thingies,' said Johnny. 'And Sam said if we're good, we can do it again sometime.'

'Did he now?' said Dad, rubbing their heads. 'Not too soon though, eh, I don't think my heart could stand another event like this.' He turned to Sam, hand out at the ready. 'Thank you,' he said, 'I can't tell you how grateful I am.'

'Huh hum,' coughed Pete.

'And the same goes for you,' said Dad. 'I'm sure you did your bit as well.' He looked around for the rest of the rescue team. 'Where are the others?'

'They decided to stop up there and get a bit of practice in,' said Sam. 'We climbers can be a dedicated lot when we want to be.'

Tammy appeared at my side. 'Told you,' she said. 'At least we can get back to enjoying ourselves now.'

I couldn't help but let out a little laugh. What was it about siblings?

'I do love them,' she added, 'but I also know what they're like.'

We stood watching the scene before us: Mum almost in tears, such was her relief; Dad not far behind even if he would never admit it; Sam and Pete, the proud heroes of the hour; and the twins, excitedly talking over each other as they described their experience down to the last detail. And although not quite sure whether it was due to my own sense of relief at Luke and Johnny being found safe and sound, or, indeed, what had gone on during this holiday in its entirety, I suddenly felt a bit overwhelmed.

'I'll be back in a minute,' I said to Tammy, leaving everyone to it.

I slipped outside for some fresh air and, taking in the fabulous view, I found myself contemplating what a rollercoaster ride this trip had been so far. The ride I knew was only going to get worse thanks to this wedding, no matter how confident the others were in their determination to pull it off.

How could you be so stupid? I thought about all the trouble *I'd* caused, never mind Luke and Johnny. Not just for me but for everyone.

'You okay?' said a voice from behind.

I turned to see Sam joining me.

'Yeah, I'm fine,' I replied. 'Just enjoying the view.'

'Gorgeous, isn't it?'

We stood there for a moment, soaking up the atmosphere.

'Thanks for today,' I said. 'I dread to think what would've happened to those two if you hadn't been here.'

'It looks scarier up there than it actually is,' he said.

I laughed. 'If you know what you're doing, maybe.'

I turned to look at him. Despite his scheming and game playing, I guessed there was quite a nice guy in there somewhere. And thinking about our relationship so far, I had to concede not many men knew how to save lives *and* put a romantic picnic together. Oh yes, there was definitely more to this chap than met the eye.

'What?' he asked, meeting my gaze.

Without thinking, I leaned up and quickly kissed him, surprising myself as much as him. But for some reason I couldn't stop there and I kissed him again, only this time I let my lips linger for that little bit longer.

Our eyes remained transfixed and my heart began to race as I suddenly felt his arms wrap around me, our lips meeting once more and with such a gentle passion I thought I would melt. And in that moment, I didn't just want it to go on forever, I completely forgot the rest of the world around us.

'Grandma! Grandma!' two little voices excitedly sang out. 'Aunty Lydia and Sam are kissing!'

I immediately pulled away.

'I'm sorry,' I said, embarrassed. 'I shouldn't have done that.'

Jesus! What was I thinking?

CHAPTER EIGHTEEN

The good lad always knows of an alternate path.

'It was a gratitude kiss,' I said, getting my bag ready for the day ahead. 'Nothing more, nothing less.'

Apparently having forgotten I was the Queen of Queens when it came to list making, Mum had called around to check I'd made a note of everything I needed to pick up from Kos. At least that was the reason she gave for her impromptu visit. However, due to the fact that she'd talked more about Sam than anything else since landing, I now began to suspect otherwise.

'That's not how Luke and Johnny describe it,' she said.

'They're eight years old,' I replied. 'What else can you expect from kids that age?'

'But you make such a lovely couple.'

'Says who?'

She let out a wistful sigh.

I stopped what I was doing. 'Mum, we might be in Greece, but this isn't *Mama Mia*, *My Big Fat Greek Wedding* or *Shirley Valentine*, is it? This is real life. So whatever love story you've got planned, I suggest you just forget it.'

A horn beeped outside. Not quite saved by the bell, but certainly as good as in my book.

Mum got up to have a look while I gathered the last of my things together.

'Very nice,' she said. 'Looks like you'll be travelling in style.'

'Really,' I replied, thinking back to the last time he'd come to collect me. Although with us about to embark on a shopping trip to beat all shopping trips, how on earth we were going to manage on two wheels was something I preferred not to think about.

'Good job you got all dressed up.'

I caught my reflection in the glass as I headed for the door, wondering if she was being sarcastic or if I had really overdone it on the attire front? 'I'm nothing of the sort,' I said, ignoring her knowing smile.

'Have fun!'

'I'll try,' I called back. 'And make sure you lock up behind you.'

I got to the bottom of the steps and suddenly stopped dead in my tracks. With no scooter in sight it appeared Mum hadn't been exaggerating in her observations at all. Instead of balancing on his usual ride, Sam sat in a very flash car indeed. Big, black and shiny, I could already see its plush cream leather seats. In fact, everything about the vehicle, from its paint job to its alloys, screamed expensive. And as I hazarded a guess the car wasn't his, one of the perks of the job more like, I couldn't help but think he certainly looked the part even it was only borrowed.

He glanced at me in return, jumped out and raced around to the passenger door. He opened it for me and leaned in to plant a kiss on my cheek.

I managed to dodge it before it landed. As far as I was concerned, there'd been enough of that behaviour already.

'Your carriage awaits,' he said, his initial sparkle now gone—a carriage that I quickly found to be just as showy on the inside as it was on the out.

I pretended not to see his disappointment. 'How do you understand all this?' I asked instead, the dashboard resembling an aeroplane cockpit with all its electronic displays.

'Things aren't always as complicated as they seem,' he said, and I could tell by his tone this was a dig of some sort, but being way to cryptic for me I chose to overlook it.

The drive down to Pothia was tense. The two of us might not always have seen eye to eye on things, but we'd never been stuck for words before. There'd always been some sort of banter flitting between us, as well as the odd proper conversation. Now, though, as I tried to come up with something to say, everything sounded forced in my mind.

All thanks to that kiss, I realised, hanging in the air like some giant pink elephant.

I knew I should bring it up, get it out of the way. But how could I do that when I still wasn't sure how I personally felt about it?

Yes, it was a wonderful kiss as kisses go. In fact, despite what I'd told my mother, a part of me wouldn't have minded experiencing it again, if only to see if I went all weak at the knees the second time around. On the other hand, another part of me kept insisting the whole episode had been wrong from the start.

I'd never gone in for flings, holiday or otherwise, and when it came to anything more serious, Sam wasn't the one for me. Of course, on top of all that there was the embarrassment factor to consider. After all, not usually so forward, I was the one who'd instigated it.

I snuck a sideward glance his way, only to find him doing the same with me. And as both of us quickly flushed red and faced forward, it was clear we were both feeling uncomfortable.

This is going to be one hell of a day, I thought, as we continued our way in yet more silence.

Arriving at the harbour, Sam jumped out to buy a ticket before returning and driving us onto the boat. A lot bigger than the vessel I'd sailed into Kalymnos on, the *Zeus* was more than capable of taking vehicles, unlike the Dolphin which had been for foot passengers only. But even then, manoeuvring proved tricky, although Sam handled it well enough. He'd obviously driven the car before.

'Shall we?' he said, turning the engine off.

We got out and began making our way up to the deck.

'You look nice,' he said, at last finding his voice even if he did come across a bit formal.

'Thank you,' I replied, at last finding mine. 'So do you.' A little more groomed and tidier than usual, he'd obviously gone to some effort.

The wind was getting up so we found a seat in a quiet corner and I began taking in our surroundings. The view out to sea was as gorgeous as ever and there were lots of tourists on board, some with suitcases, clicking away on their cameras to chart their last moments here before heading off somewhere else. I'd have got mine out too given half the chance, but it didn't seem right considering the mood surrounding Sam and me. Holiday snapshots should be all sunshine and smiles, not a record of the unease we were experiencing. On the plus side, though, at least things could only get better.

Vibrations started to trickle through my feet as the boat raised its anchor and began to move.

'About the other day,' said Sam.

My stomach lurched. I should've known he wouldn't be able to leave it. But it was one thing needing this conversation and quite another to actually have it.

'What about it?' I replied.

He looked me directly in the eyes and my stomach did another summersault. 'You tell me,' he said.

The intenseness of his stare felt quite disconcerting and I shifted uncomfortably, for some reason suddenly needing to clear my throat. 'There's nothing to tell. It should never have happened.'

Disappointment flashed across his face—something I hadn't expected from a game player like him—and I felt the need to explain.

'Sam, I don't do holiday romances, you should know that by now. As for anything more, it's pretty obvious we're not right for each other.' I let out a half-hearted laugh.

'I'm not the man on your list, you mean?' He was deadly serious.

'No,' I replied. 'You're not.'

I thought back to that darned kiss almost wishing he could be my Prince Charming, before quickly pulling myself together again. It was clear that if either of us were harbouring any notions of taking things further, now was the time to put things straight.

'I've invested so much in this guy, Sam. A guy who you, along with everyone else, probably thinks doesn't exist. And, yes, you might all be right in the long run. But I'm not ready to settle for anyone else just yet and if that sounds harsh I'm sorry. It's just the way it is.'

He shrugged, slumping back in his seat as if at a loss.

'Can't we just be friends?' I said. 'Go over to Kos and have a fun day like friends would?'

I held my breath while he thought for a moment. Surely, he knew we had enough on our plates having to organise things for Katerina's wedding without a complication like this as well.

'Okay,' he replied, finally coming around to a more sensible way of thinking, even if he did sound a tad reluctant. 'Why not?'

'Great!' I began rooting in my bag, eventually pulling out my camera. 'Now stand over there and for goodness sake—smile.'

As we neared Kos, everyone around us jumped out of their seats ready to race ashore the second we docked in Mastihari. And remembering the last time I was caught up in such a melee, I made sure we held back. Besides, as we took a more leisurely descent down to the car deck, there wasn't any point in us rushing. We couldn't go anywhere until the vehicle in front moved on, something the locals didn't realise.

'So how do you want to play this?' asked Sam, as we jumped in and buckled up.

'We should probably get the shopping out of the way first and then maybe have some lunch,' I replied.

'And if we have time after that I could always show you the sights?' he said.

'Have you seen how much stuff we need to pick up today?' I asked. 'Lugging it all around isn't exactly going to be easy.'

Other vehicles began to disembark and we followed them off the boat. We took a left, and the drive into Kos turned out to be pleasant enough. Just one long road and roughly thirty minutes later we were there and parked up.

'Coffee?' suggested Sam.

We headed for Eleftheria Square—a large area lined with old, imposing buildings and an archaeological museum. According to Sam, there was even an ancient mosque and an old bathhouse turned into a café somewhere in the vicinity.

It was the numerous coffee bars that gave the place its modern feel and I'd have loved to sit under one of the giant umbrellas for a while just people watching. But without any time for that, we simply picked one of the establishments at random and took a seat. Sam called out to the waiter and impressively ordered our drinks in Greek, while I dug my shopping list out and began to scan its contents.

'So, we definitely need table linen,' I said, getting straight to it. 'And because it's an evening wedding and we don't have a lot of time to sort out fancy decorations, I thought the easiest and most simple way forward is to play with the lighting. You know, lanterns for the tables, candles etcetera, and maybe some fairy lights for the vines. You'll have no problem putting them up, being a handyman and all that, will you? What do you think?'

I looked up to find Sam staring at me, amused.

'What?'

'Do you do everything in lists?'

'Everything,' I replied.

The waiter came over with a couple of frappés and I took a sip, automatically flinching at the taste.

'You don't like it?' asked Sam.

'Nope. There's something intrinsically wrong when it comes to cold coffee.'

He appeared confused. 'But I have seen you drink them before, haven't I?'

'Of course you have,' I replied. 'When in Rome and all that.'

He shook his head, as if to say this was yet one more thing he'd never understand about me, while I got on with prioritising our purchases.

'I must say, you're handling this wedding thing pretty well, considering,' he said.

'Considering the hot mess we're going to make of it, you mean?' I replied.

'There is that, I suppose. But I'm talking about how well you're dealing with it emotionally, you know?'

I put my list down. 'There isn't a lot else I can do, is there? Yes, I could sit here crying and telling myself this should be me getting married. In fact, I almost did when we were round at yours the other day. But having dug myself into a very big hole the way I have, I've just got to concentrate on getting myself out of it. With a little help from lots of other people like you, of course.' A gust of wind got up and I shivered, wishing I'd brought a cardigan with me. 'Anyway,' I added, 'we're always talking about me. Tell me something about you for a change.'

He shifted in his seat. Ever the joker, he clearly didn't like being the centre of attention when it came to anything remotely serious. 'I've already said there's nothing to tell.'

'International man of mystery, eh?'

'If only you knew.' He got up from his seat. 'Come on, we've got shopping to do.'

We spent the next couple of hours wandering up and down the cobbled streets in search of everything we needed, visiting this and that shop, ticking items off our list when we found them. Sam could be quite the drill sergeant when he wanted to be. 'We're not here for that,' he said, when a jewellery store window caught my eye. 'We haven't got time for this,' he informed me when I paused to admire a particularly nice range of shoes. However, I didn't intend on going home completely empty-handed on the personal front. And even though he mostly kept us on track, I did manage to pick up a couple of extras along the way—only the most beautiful pair of sandals I'd ever seen and an absolutely to-die-for print sarong.

Laden with bags, we finally plonked ourselves down on a bench ready for a well-earned rest.

'We have got everything, haven't we?' I asked. With the shops due to close for the afternoon siesta, I really didn't fancy having to start traipsing around again later in the evening.

'It looks that way,' said Sam, consulting the list one last time.

My feet ached from all the walking we'd done and I leaned down to rub my ankles. 'So, what now?'

'I think we should hit the tourist trail,' he said. 'We might as well get as much in as we can while we're here.'

I sighed, both my feet and I having anticipated him suggesting a leisurely late lunch, before an equally leisurely drive back to Mastihari and a relaxing sail back to Kalymnos.

'Come on,' he said, up and off the bench before I could protest.

He was a man far too active for his own good let alone mine, so I remained seated, wondering how long it would take him to realise I wasn't actually following.

It took a few moments but he fathomed it eventually, stopped in his tracks, turned and came back again. 'Okay, so you don't want to do the whole tourist thing. But there's this one place we just have to visit,' he said.

I eyed him suspiciously.

'You won't be disappointed,' he promised. 'See it as developing your cultural side.'

'So, you're saying I'm not cultured enough, are you?' I replied.

'No, not at all. I'm saying this is one sight you'll be glad you didn't miss.'

I doubted that very much; however, as he was so keen we should go I hauled myself onto my very reluctant feet regardless. 'Come on then,' I said, gathering up my share of the shopping bags. 'What're we waiting for?'

We made our way towards the harbour, eventually passing through a vault-like archway.

'Ta daa!' said Sam, as we came out the other side.

I could see it wasn't the entrance to the castle he was applauding, but more what stood in front of it—a hollow tree, its branches propped up with poles, the whole thing in the middle of an enclosure, obviously designed to stop the likes of us getting too close. Faced with nothing but wood, it proved difficult to conjure up the required enthusiasm, a fact that didn't go unnoticed.

'This isn't just any old tree, you know,' Sam explained. 'It's a plane tree.'

Like that makes any difference.

'Supposedly the largest in Europe,' he carried on. He took me by the arm and pulled me closer. 'It's the tree of Hippocrates. The man himself is said to have sat under it while he taught his students the art of medicine. Not this actual one of course, this is only around five hundred years old. But it is supposed to be a descendant of the original.' He gazed at it with such awe. 'Just imagine what it must have been like back then.'

He spoke with such gusto that I couldn't help but smile; his eagerness reminded me of Luke and Johnny every time we visited the zoo. Moreover, Hippocrates might not have been my thing, but I was certainly seeing a new side to Sam. He clearly had more to him than I'd given him credit for and I wondered what else he'd kept hidden.

He pulled out his mobile and I watched him set it to camera before tapping the shoulder of the guy standing next to him. 'Would you mind?' he asked, handing it over. 'One for the album and all that.' He arranged us both in front of the tree and indicated that we were ready. One click later, the job was done. 'Cheers, mate,' he said, retrieving his phone.

We looked at the image. Sam appeared happy and relaxed, handsome even. Unfortunately for me though, it wasn't exactly my finest hour photograph-wise.

'Jesus,' I said. 'You're gonna have to delete that!'

'Why? You look gorgeous,' said Sam—something he obviously actually believed.

'And you need glasses,' I replied.

He tucked his phone safely away so I couldn't get at it. 'I'd suggest we have a look around the castle but I don't think we have time, do we?'

I espied the seating area in a nearby café. 'And I'd suggest we have a drink. Although you're right, I suppose we should call it a day.'

Thankfully, the walk to the car wasn't too bad, Sam playing the gentleman and carrying most of the shopping along the way. The drive back to Mastihari brought a welcome relief and not just for my aching feet; it had been a long day. I was tired full stop and I just wanted to get home to relax. More to the point, with only forty-eight hours to the wedding, tonight would be my only chance to chill a little before activities really kicked in. Tomorrow was all about preparing the Fatolitis' bar ready for its transformation.

'That's strange,' said Sam as we pulled up at the little port, 'the ferry should be here by now.'

I checked my watch. 'It could be running late.'

The group of people waiting at the docking area told us we hadn't missed it, that it must still be on its way over. But it was nowhere in sight.

'Maybe it's not coming,' I said, taking in the swell of the ocean.

'It does look pretty choppy out there, doesn't it?' said Sam.

We got out of the car for a closer look, immediately feeling the gusts of wind whipping around our ears.

'What're we going to do?' I asked. 'We can't stop here. Not with a wedding to sort out asap.'

Sam approached the other would-be passengers in the hope of finding out what was happening.

'It's okay,' he said, giving me an update. 'They've already contacted the pirate boat.'

'Pirate boat?' I asked.

'The chap who takes people over when the official ferries stop running.'

I took another glimpse at the sea before me. 'When it's too dangerous, you mean?'

Sam laughed. 'Don't look so scared. People use it all the time.'

'But what about the car?' I asked.

'We'll have to leave it here. I'll come back for it tomorrow.'

I wasn't convinced.

'You do want to get back, don't you?' he said.

I realised I didn't have much of a choice. However, even as the pirate boat appeared on the horizon, I still wasn't sure we were doing the right thing.

'What the…?'

A screeching car appeared as if from nowhere and sped down the concrete jetty towards us. Even worse, as it came to a screaming halt, I watched on in horror as two guys jumped out, raced around to the boot and hastily grabbed two large containers of fluid from within. All the while, they seemed to be checking their surroundings to make sure they hadn't been seen.

Trying to maintain a degree of anonymity was a fruitless exercise in my view, taking into account their very loud and conspicuous arrival. Nevertheless, it soon became clear that the name 'pirate boat' was actually a pseudonym for illegal; the two men were providing fuel for the return journey.

I felt like I was in some sort of action movie as the captain hastily took everyone's cash and ushered us all on board. Quite a task taking into consideration all of our baggage as well—some with suitcases, a chap with a heavy-looking sack of all things, and Sam and me with our shopping. And with the captain also frantically checking that the authorities weren't around to witness these events, the sense of urgency about the whole thing was palpable to the point that I wondered what on earth we were doing.

The boat looked safe enough, I noted, and at about thirty feet in length there was plenty of room. But before we could settle ourselves, the engines roared into action and we were suddenly off; I was almost flung into the air in the process.

'Don't worry,' said Sam, helping me steady myself.

Boy did I hate it when he said things like that.

I glanced about at the other passengers who'd clearly done this trip before, chatting away unperturbed. As the boat got further out to sea, some conversations desisted, as holding on for dear life became more of a priority.

The boat bounced on the surf—flying up into the air before crashing back down again. Every wave we hit felt like we were being slammed against a brick wall. People were being thrown this way and the other, and as if that wasn't enough, it felt like the boat was about to snap in two at any given moment. Then what would happen to us?

We all clung to our belongings, the chap with the sack unable to maintain his grip. And as the hessian landed in an uncontrollable heap, its contents were revealed—the front end of a dead sheep was just what we needed. *Jesus.* Its beady eyes stared right at me as it slid closer. Although with water being thrown at us from all angles by what felt like the bucketful, my attention was soon diverted again. In fact, the cynical side of me marvelled at people paying good money for fear-inducing rides like this, although I didn't think the Log Flume at Alton Towers actually compared.

I looked at Sam, convinced we were going to die. His returning, reassuring smile told me we weren't.

Naturally, I didn't believe him for one second. Still, at least on this occasion if I was going overboard, he was coming with me. Not much of a consolation in the bigger scheme of things, I had to admit, but at least it was something.

CHAPTER NINETEEN

A walking stick in a corner, therefore it's raining.

'I'm telling you. The man is trying to kill me.'

While he headed back to Kos to collect his boss's car, Mum and I sat in Sam's kitchen attempting to peel a great mound of potatoes. A mound that didn't appear to be getting any smaller no matter how many we got through.

'First, he tried to knock me out with a football,' I explained, much to my mother's amusement. 'Which didn't just blooming well hurt, it sent me flying across the beach.'

'An accident like that could happen to anyone,' she said and, as she continued to chuckle, I could see she was telling herself this was probably just another one of my exaggerations.

But when it came to Sam what else was I supposed to think? Every time I was with him something detrimental to my physical well-being happened. And next time I might not be so lucky.

'Then he insists I trek into the middle of goodness knows where and almost causes me to break my ankle,' I carried on, 'and that was after the scooter ride from hell.'

Mum looked down at my scantily sandalled feet. 'And what shoes did you happen to be wearing at the time?'

'And to top it all off, there's the escapade on the high seas that he put me through and I can't begin to tell you how frightening that was.' I paused in my peeling. 'The force we kept hitting those waves with was terrifying, Mum. My bones are still vibrating today because of it.'

'So, Sam's responsible for the weather as well now, is he?'

I looked at her, flabbergasted. Did she not hear all the examples I'd just given? Could this man do *any* wrong?

'Plus, there's the stress of being a blackmail victim. You do know stress can cause cancer, don't you?'

'The way I see it,' Mum replied, 'you've brought most of this so-called stress on yourself.'

I rolled my eyes as I tackled another spud. In this particular instance, her observation may have been right, but that didn't mean I wanted to hear it.

'Anyway,' she continued, 'I think he's a nice guy. And if you weren't so set in your ways when it came to these things you'd see that too. Look at the way he and your dad got stuck in with painting the bar yesterday. He didn't have to, did he? But because he cares about his friends…'

'Of course, I know he's a nice guy… sometimes. But every time I think like that, he goes and does something to ruin it. And unlike Luke and Johnny I only have one life to play with and it's one I'd like to keep living, thank you very much.

'What are you talking about, anyway?' I added. 'I'm not set in my ways.'

A key in the door cut our conversation short—speak of the devil.

'Are my ears burning?' asked Sam, as he and Dad made their entrance. He casually threw his keys on the side.

'Only in a good way,' replied Mum.

I lifted my eyes to the heavens once more. 'Like we don't have better things to talk about.'

Mum glanced behind them. 'Where's everyone else?' she asked.

'They decided to walk,' replied Dad.

'What? All the way up that hill?' I laughed. 'I'd pay good money to see that.'

'I think Pete's hoping to burn off some of Luke and Johnny's excess energy,' said Sam. 'They're a bit excited about tonight.'

The wedding. I'd been so busy with the preparations I hadn't concentrated on what all this effort was actually for. Still, there was no time to dwell on that now, what with all the stuff we had to sort out. Like putting up the decorations for the bar, let alone preparing all this food.

'You two get off,' said Mum, as if reading my mind. She referred to the notepad on the table next to her, having organised a timetable of what had to be completed and by what time, all down to the most minute detail. 'We can manage here until you're done, can't we, Dad?'

She took my knife and offered it to my father, who much to my surprise simply sat down and rolled his sleeves up. I'd never seen him peel a potato in my whole life and watching him happy to just get on with it was definitely a new experience. *Wow, all this sea air must really be getting to him.*

Of course, he wasn't the only one who didn't need telling twice. My hands felt shrivelled to the point of no return because of all the potato starch and I was more than willing to let him take over.

'Come on then,' I said to Sam, giving my hands a quick rinse under the tap before drying them with the tea towel. 'Let's get to it.'

Once outside, Sam threw me a scooter helmet.

'Do we have to go on that?' I asked, catching it.

'I'm afraid so,' he replied. 'The car needs to stay here ready to be loaded up.'

I supposed he had a point and climbing on behind him I told myself that at least on this occasion we weren't going far. And I got my wish of seeing Pete struggling up the hill behind my more mobile little nephews; my brother's red, sweaty face brought a smile to mine as we passed them by.

Cruel of me, I know.

We pulled up outside the Fatolitis' and I had to admit I was impressed. Sam had done a pretty decent paint job on the place. Just how he'd managed to rope my dad into helping I had no idea. Short of putting a rocket up his backside, we Livingstons couldn't get the head of the household to do anything remotely physical, yet this man had succeeded in getting him up a ladder.

I glanced around. Without the posters and climbing shoes, the freshly whitewashed walls provided a great canvas to work with. And because Sam and Dad had even cleaned the whole establishment, it was just a case of us getting stuck into the fun part—turning a bog-standard bar into a beautiful wedding venue.

Sam and I worked well together. I gave instructions as to where he should hang the fairy lights and lanterns and place the candles, and he followed my orders to the letter.

Mum had already explained about how Greek dancing was an important contribution to any Hellenic celebration, so making sure to leave a space for this, we organised the tables into the pre-planned formation. And even though I still wasn't sure about placing the bride's and groom's seats under the noose that Sam and Dad had conveniently forgotten to take down, I went with it. Sam's delight at their little in-joke was something I couldn't ignore.

We moved on to laying the tables, shining each item of cutlery and wiping each wine glass as we went. The little glass vases and vibrant cerise daisies didn't just make simple yet beautiful centre pieces, but contrasted with the brilliant white linen perfectly. However, having got up at the crack of dawn to get them all pressed and ironed, I'd have been happy if I never saw a tablecloth or napkin ever again

We finished up by sprinkling a handful of pink diamante hearts around each setting and then stood back to admire our handiwork.

'What do you think?' I asked, taking it all in.

'You wouldn't think it was the same place, would you?' said Sam.

He was genuinely in awe of what we'd achieved and I surprised myself when I realised his opinion actually mattered to me.

'You've certainly got an eye for this kind of thing,' he said, putting an arm around the back of my shoulders. 'The bride is going to love it.'

'I can't wait to see what it looks like with all the candles and lights going as well,' I said, looking forward to the spectacle. 'And I hope you're right about Katerina. Fingers crossed, it'll make up for the catering side of things.'

Nearby business owners began arriving with their microwaves and it was nice to see them impressed with what we'd achieved as well.

'*Pollee Oraia…* Very nice,' said one.

'Bravo, bravo,' said another.

And so the compliments kept coming.

I stood back to let Sam direct them all through to the kitchen, hoping against all hope that we'd be able to pull tonight off.

'You have nothing to worry about,' said Sam, reading my face. 'Honestly.' And with the last of the locals disappearing, he rejoined me.

'I know we still have lots more to do up at the house, but after all that, do you want me to call down here before I go to the church?' he asked.

His question threw me.

'The church?'

'Where else would I be going?' he said. 'That is where weddings take place around here.'

It took a second for his words to sink in; but of course, Sam would be attending the ceremony. He and the Fatolitis had been friends for years by all accounts, so quite rightly he'd be invited. It was just that he'd done such a good job so far with the preparations and had been on hand every step of the way, I'd automatically got it into my head he'd be a part of the team to the very end.

'You don't have to do that,' I said, trying to keep my disappointment in check.

'I know I don't,' he said. 'I want to.'

Our eyes locked just long enough for us both to notice.

'You might not have time,' I said, dismissing the moment. 'For all we know, we could be peeling vegetables until the eleventh hour.' I made a point of returning my attention to the tables.

'Will this lot be all right with us just leaving it like this? Won't someone come along and spoil it?'

Sam laughed at my concern. 'Of course, it'll be all right. This is Kalymnos.'

As we made our way back to the house, I almost dreaded what we would find. Mum might be an expert when it came to cooking a Livingston Sunday lunch, but a Sunday lunch for fifty Greek strangers is a whole different ball game.

I needn't have worried though; we were met with an organised hive of activity. Well-deserved cup of tea in hand, Mum had everything and everyone suitably under control.

Tammy was putting the finishing touches to a production line of cheesecakes; Luke, Johnny and Pete were packing cooked vegetables into giant Tupperware boxes, and Dad stood at the stove conscientiously stirring a large vat of soup.

'I'm impressed,' I said.

An alarm clock began to sound and Mum jumped up. 'That'll be the meat,' she said, grabbing a tea towel ready to take the beef out of the oven.

As she set it down to rest, I began to salivate just looking at it.

'Very nice,' said Sam. 'And it smells wonderful, Mrs Livingston.'

She shot him a look, as if to tell him she'd told him before.

'Sorry,' he said. 'I mean it smells wonderful, *Margot*.'

He opened a drawer and pulled out a set of keys. 'You'll need these, Pete,' he said, tossing them over.

'Cheers, mate,' said my brother, trying and failing to control his excitement.

'You've got to be kidding me,' I said. 'You're letting *him* drive the car?'

'Why wouldn't I?' asked Sam.

'Yes, why wouldn't he?' echoed Pete.

'We've got to get this food down to the Fatolitis somehow,' said Mum—a task I'd previously and wrongly assumed Sam would be undertaking.

'And do your bosses know about this?' I asked.

My question was met with silence.

'I thought not.'

They all stared at me like I was some kind of bad guy.

'Well, if he damages it in any way, don't say I didn't warn you.'

I turned to my father.

'And if he does, Dad, I'm letting you know now that I'm *not* footing the bill.'

'He won't,' said Dad.

'I won't,' said Pete.

CHAPTER TWENTY

The donkey called the rooster big-headed.

After stalling the car a couple of times on the way, Pete had dropped me at my apartment before taking himself and the rest of the Livingstons back to their hotel. The plan was for us all to meet up at our pre-arranged time down at the Fatolitis.

I looked at myself in the mirror, not for the first time realising how seriously Mum was taking our role in this event; she now even insisted we wear a uniform of sorts, having provided us all with black bottoms and white tops picked up especially for the occasion.

My little skirt and cotton blouse looked pleasant enough in an upstairs downstairs kind of way. In fact, the only thing spoiling the ensemble was the fear in my eyes, something I considered quite understandable given the undertaking we were about to embark on.

So much could go wrong and so easily.

What had we been thinking?

Although going back to the very start of this fiasco, I realised it was more a case of what had *I* been thinking?

It's too late for regrets now. You just have to get on with it and hope for the best.

But who was I kidding?

I put my hand on my stomach, the enormity of what lay ahead starting to make me feel sick to the point that I didn't think I could go through with it. Not that I really had the luxury of walking away, however tempting it might seem.

Come on, Lydia, you don't have time for this. You've got no choice but to finish what you started.

Besides, wasn't everyone else confident enough? Especially Mum and she'd been the one bearing the heaviest responsibility of sorting out the food. So, if she could get through this then surely, I could, too.

But the situation was more complicated for me, wasn't it?

I heard an engine roaring outside. Thankfully the distraction prevented me from getting too morbid.

Pete! No doubt dropping Mum, Tammy and the boys off, which of course only meant one thing—it was now make-or-break time.

'Right, Lydia Livingston, here goes,' I said, pulling myself together and putting on my best smile. Although as these things go, even I could see it wasn't a very convincing one.

With nothing else for it, I left my reflection behind and headed for the door. By the time I got down to the Fatolitis, Dad and Pete were already driving off into the distance, I assumed to continue ferrying things from the house to here.

'Oh, Lydia, this is beautiful,' said Mum, taking in the place's transformation. 'Just stunning.'

I had to smile at her response, wondering if that really was a tear in her eye. 'Thanks, Mum,' I replied. 'My years of planning finally paid off, eh?'

She put her arm around me. 'They certainly have... But we can talk about all that later, love. For now, we've got work to do.'

She allowed herself one last wistful sigh before directing us all into the kitchen and as I watched her studying her lists, I thoroughly admired the way she'd thrown herself into this, the way she relished the challenge.

'Tammy, can you clear this area for the food containers, please? Luke and Johnny, if you two could start lining up the soup bowls. And Lydia, if you could light the stove, that would be much appreciated.'

There was quite an air of excited anticipation among us by the time the food was unloaded and organised, Mum having already given us all our instructions. Tammy, Dad and Pete would be serving; Luke and Johnny, bless them, had the task of counting out the crockery in numbers of five to match the five microwaves; and it was my job, being head chef in name only, to assist the real woman in charge to plate up. All we had to do now was wait.

We watched as the band arrived and set up near the dance area, shortly followed by the bar staff who'd been drafted in for the night, and then the baker with the wedding cake—a beautifully constructed four-tiered affair, iced in white and adorned with a garland of pink roses that swept down one side—just exquisite.

'The candles! Quick, get me a match or something.' Realising they hadn't been lit yet, I set about the final stage of the space's transformation.

I raced over to the plug socket. 'Now for the *pièce de résistance*,' I said, flicking the switch.

'Wow!' said Luke and Johnny.

'Oh, my word,' said Mum.

'It's like something out of a fairy tale,' said Tammy.

Even Dad and my brother appeared awestruck.

'You've done them proud, sis,' said Pete.

He was right, I had. It was more than beautiful. To me it was perfect. 'Thanks, guys,' I said, almost welling up. Thank goodness for the car horns suddenly beeping or I really would've been in a state.

The band leader called over to us. 'They're on their way,' he said. Incessant horn honking was obviously part of the celebrations.

'Right, everyone,' said Mum. 'Action stations, please.'

'Hang on! Just a minute,' said Pete, racing out to the kitchen before quickly returning with a buttonhole. He frantically pinned it to himself, making sure it dangled upside down in the process. 'What?' he asked the rest of us who were wondering what on earth he was doing. 'Sam suggested I wear it. You put them upside down to let other guests know you're single.'

Mum shook her head, at the same time ushering Luke, Johnny and me into the kitchen. While she set the soup to boil, stirring all the while, and my nephews set about counting bowls out into rows of five, I had no choice but to just stand there and wait for them to finish up.

I took the opportunity to peek at what was happening outside. Numerous cars were parking and guests were now making their entrance. Dad, Pete and Tammy looked quite the part as they showed people to their seats, pouring them a glass of wine as they did so, and I was pleased to note many of them admiring the bar's radical alterations—at this rate, anyone would think we were a professional outfit.

I saw Sam arriving and, as he nodded my way and gave me a little wink, my tummy did a little summersault. Sam looked quite dapper compared to his usual self. I had never seen him in a suit before and it was obvious the man scrubbed up well. He'd pulled his hair back into a neat ponytail and although he hadn't had a full shave, his stubble had certainly been groomed. *Very nice.*

'Wait for me,' a female voice called out.

Soulla appeared at his side and, much to my disappointment, looked very elegant. In fact, the two of them appeared quite the couple the way she draped herself around him and I wouldn't have been surprised if their buttonholes were suddenly sitting upright come the end of the evening. But what did I care anyway?

Another car pulled up; the proud family of the bride at last made their entrance. Tammy almost tripped as she ran to their aid in a bid to show them to their seats. I could see it was Yiannis she really wanted to get close to, her eyes twinkling even more as it became apparent he was equally delighted to see her in return.

'You are young,' I said, the cynical side of me coming to the fore, 'but you will learn.'

Suddenly the band leader was talking over his mic and everyone rose to their feet to hail the arrival of the happy couple.

This is it, I thought, as Katerina got out of the car looking every inch the angel she'd predicted.

Her dress was simple yet stunning. Ivory and not white, it sat off the shoulder and had the most elaborately embroidered sleeves; fitted down to the waistline, its skirt fell loose with just the right amount of train.

She put her hand up to her chest; the bar's transformation appeared to take her breath away and I couldn't help but smile. But just as quickly her attention diverted to her guests and, of course, her new husband, who had so much love in his eyes as he proudly showed her off. He was clearly besotted and being such a handsome man, I could see why Katerina had fallen for him.

Everyone re-took their seats as the newlyweds began a walk around the dance floor, clearly a Greek tradition, with the rest of us cooing over what a fine-looking pair they made. And although I, too, enjoyed watching them, I felt a touch of sadness; I so wished this could be my special day.

'Come on, love, that's enough,' said Mum, all at once standing at my shoulder. She signalled to Dad that we were ready to go as she guided me away from the door. 'We've got work to do.'

From that point on it was all systems go in the kitchen. Luke and Johnny turned their attentions from bowls to plates, taking their role very seriously as they continued to count out in numbers of five. Mum went from stirring soup to getting a head start on plating up the main course; once she'd shown me how, I took over, enabling her to commence with the microwaving. Throughout all this, Dad, Pete and Tammy zipped in and out, keeping up with the plates as they were ready to be served. How we all managed to keep going was anyone's guess.

A couple of times I managed to sneak a glimpse out at the diners. Understandably, the Yorkshire puddings attracted a few strange looks from among the guests; however, once tasted, the crowd was pleasantly surprised. Less pleasant though was the way Sam and Soulla appeared to be getting along tonight. Laughing at his every word, she kept playing with her hair and in return he kept touching her hand.

It's all right for some. I got back to what I was supposed to be doing, in the by now hot and sweaty kitchen, the place where the hired help belonged.

'There,' said Mum, handing Tammy the last of the cheesecakes. 'Now we can relax.'

'Thank God,' replied my niece, making her exit. 'My feet are killing me.'

Hers weren't the only ones.

I wiped my hand over my brow and stared at the mountain of washing up. 'Not quite, Mum,' I said.

'We can do that,' said Luke and Johnny, eager to continue with their usefulness.

I smiled. They'd behaved so well throughout all of this, I actually felt quite proud of them for a change.

'Knock! Knock!'

I turned to see Sam in the doorway and automatically smoothed down my clothes and straightened up my hair.

'Looks like you pulled it off,' he said. 'There's quite a few happy customers out there, you know.'

'I noticed,' I replied, thinking of one woman in particular.

'Katerina wondered if you wanted to come and join the *Koumeres*?'

Like I know what that means.

Sam laughed, picking up on my ignorance. 'The *Koumeres* are the best women. Yes, they do have best women here and not only that, why have one when you can have five? Anyway, they're about to get up and dance and the bride would like you to join them.'

Again, I tidied my hair. As if I was going to go anywhere near that Soulla woman looking like this.

'It's quite an honour…' he coaxed.

'I don't think so,' I said, 'we still have work to do.'

'What if I said you get to dance with the *Koumbari*? Would that be enough to change your mind?'

'Don't tell me. The best men?'

'Of which I am one.'

Mum looked at me as if to say I should.

'I'll tell you what, you lot do the dancing and I'll watch. How's that?'

Both Sam and Mum looked disappointed by my decision, but I told myself at least Soulla would be happy.

'While I'm helping the others clear the rest of the tables,' I added, just in case he had designs of roping me in regardless.

The *Koumares* and *Koumbari* dance began civilized enough, the women getting up first to commence the proceedings. Once the chaps joined in though, things began to get a little more raucous, with the whole thing culminating in a display of acrobatics. I watched as the groom was lifted off his feet and hurled into the air over and over again. Images of untimely visits to the local hospital entered my mind as he was tossed about like a pancake. However, everyone else found the spectacle great fun and thankfully it ended without incident.

As I carried on collecting anything and everything that needed washing up, the music changed key, signalling the start of a slow little number that left the bride and groom deserted on the dance floor. Finally, they came together to whisper sweet nothings and gaze into each other's eyes. Talk about romantic. I looked around, wondering if everyone else found the scene as dreamy as I did, at the same time spotting Soulla murmuring something in Sam's ear. If I'd been nearer, I'd have been tempted to accidentally on purpose tip something onto her lap, but I wasn't. So, I simply turned away instead.

The guests around me began fumbling in their pockets and purses for Euro notes, each of them getting up to attach their gift to the couple's clothing. Watching, I couldn't help but think the extra cash would, no doubt, come in handy at a time like this. But as I saw the happy couple wince, it was obvious a hoard of people coming at them with pins in their hands wasn't necessarily worth the pay-off.

Dad, Pete, Tammy and I finally headed back to the kitchen with the last of the washing up. Luke and Johnny had hardly made a dent on what was already there but they didn't notice or care.

'At last,' I said. 'We're done.'

Tammy's eyes lit up; she was ready to do a runner.

'Go on then,' said Mum. 'Off you go.'

She ran out of the room like a shot in search of Yiannis, almost bumping into Efthimeos as he came in.

'Lydia,' he said, and, starting with me, he immediately launched into a round of cheek kissing. 'How can I thank you all? Everything was wonderful.' He clicked his fingers and a barman appeared with a tray of generously filled brandy glasses. 'You have all worked so hard, now you relax.'

'Ooh,' said Mum. 'Just what the doctor ordered.'

'That'll do nicely,' said Dad.

'Cheers,' said Pete.

We all took a glass and sipped, ready for the Metaxa's warmth.

'Come,' said Efthimeos, indicating we should follow him. 'Come and join us.'

We left Luke and Johnny happily getting on with what they were doing, just in time to see the older generation hit the dance floor to strut their stuff, Efthimeos and Maria proudly joining in. Despite their years this lot could rock, I noted. Some of them even got down on one knee, clapping to the rhythm, by way of encouraging the others to keep at it. It was such a lovely sight, made even more fun when Mum and Dad looked at each other and decided to join in. They might not have known the moves, but they certainly gave them a good go.

The younger guests began slapping money onto their grooving elders' foreheads. Quite a strange sight, I mused, wondering what it was all about.

'This is the money dance,' said Sam, suddenly next to me. 'They call it Tipping the Band.'

'Really?' I asked. 'Why?'

'The money goes towards the band's wages,' he explained. 'The point is that the more these old timers make, the more the musicians get paid. Saves the bride and groom a fortune considering what bands like this charge these days.'

'I can imagine.'

'You look tired,' Sam continued.

'So would you if you'd just gone through what we have.'

'If I could've helped, I would've done, you know.'

'What? And miss out on gorgeous Soulla? I don't believe that for one second. I mean look, even Pete's drooling over the woman now.' Goodness knew what he was saying to her, but my brother was clearly out to impress. 'Poor lad,' I said. 'She'll eat him alive.'

'Don't tell me you're jealous,' said Sam, a thought that evidently pleased him.

I felt myself start to blush.

'You are, aren't you?'

We were distracted by a bit of a commotion out on the dance floor—a couple of younger guys seemingly taking things a little too far with the older generation.

'Shouldn't someone do something?' I asked, ready to step in myself if I had to.

'Someone will,' said Sam, completely unconcerned. 'Just watch.'

No sooner were Sam's words out than Soulla rolled up her sleeves and marched over to the troublemakers. She said something to the young men involved who immediately turned sheepish.

'She's good,' I said, not sure if I could've brought them into line quite so quickly.

Soulla was just about to walk away, however, when one of the boys decided to show off in front of his friends. He said something back, his challenge to her authority causing the rest of them to snigger. Soulla clearly wasn't happy and, after a slight pause, she swung a swift right hook—so swift her victim didn't see it coming and her fist landed clean on the guy's cheek.

Ouch! That's one way to shut him up.

He fell to the ground with such force it was debatable as to whether he'd ever get up again, leaving his friends just standing there too scared to move.

'She's *very* good,' I reassessed.

We watched her unroll her sleeves and simply walk away.

'And that's why everyone's nice to Soulla,' said Sam. 'No one dares not be.'

I made a mental note to be friendlier the next time I came into contact with her.

'So, it's got nothing to do with the fact that she's absolutely stunning, then?' After the evening's hard work, I felt positively scruffy in comparison.

'Lydia,' said Sam.

He pulled me around so we were facing each other but I couldn't bring myself to look at him.

'Surely it's obvious even to you… You're the only woman I'm interested in.'

He lifted my chin and leaned down to kiss me and with butterflies suddenly working overtime in my tummy, I closed my eyes waiting for our lips to connect.

'Thank goodness!' a rather loud voice screeched out.

My eyes opened again; Sam's lips were so near yet so far. We both turned our heads.

'You do know he's been boring me all evening because of you?' said Soulla, standing there with my desperate brother in tow. 'Lydia, this… Lydia, that…'

We looked around to see who else had been watching us. Mum, Dad, Efthimeos and Maria clearly had, the two women in the group cooing over us nearly as much as everyone had over the beautiful bride only hours earlier.

Sam and I started to giggle. We'd been so wrapped up in the moment, we hadn't realised we'd become the entertainment.

'Shall we go?' he asked.

'I think we should,' I replied.

He held my hand as we made our escape, both of us eager to pick up where we'd just left off.

Once outside, he took me in his arms and I thought I would melt into the long, lingering kiss we shared, this time without interruption. But, like all good things, it eventually came to an end.

'Fancy a nightcap at mine?' asked Sam. 'No funny business, of course.'

We'll see about that. Clearly the brandy had gone straight to my head.

'That would be lovely,' I said.

It was such a gorgeous night we decided to walk up the hill to his place, taking our time to enjoy every second of it.

'You know,' I said, thinking about the day's events. 'I can't believe we actually pulled that off… That we got away with it.'

'I can,' Sam replied.

I laughed. 'If I remember rightly, you were the one who kept insisting I should come clean with everyone.'

'Yes, but that was before your mother got involved. She's quite a woman!'

At some point on this trip, every single one of my family members had managed to surprise me in one way or another. Out of all of them though, Mum had amazed me the most. The way she'd come to my aid like that, in spite of the fact that what we were doing could have gone so, so horribly wrong. And the professionalism with which she tackled it all—that's what had really got me.

Up until now, Mum had seemed like everyone's general dogsbody, especially when it came to my dad and my brothers. I felt ashamed for not recognising her inner strength before, and I promised myself that from then on I'd show her the respect she deserved.

'She is, isn't she?' I acknowledged.

As we reached the driveway, I paused. As much as Sam had said there'd be no funny business I knew as much as he did what was probably about to happen. I felt nervous and excited at the same time and needed a second to get my head around it.

'You okay?' he asked.

I nodded. 'Yeah.'

'You know what I think,' said Sam, kissing my forehead.

My tummy tingled.

'I think what you need is a lovely, hot bath. You must be desperate for a long soak after being on your feet all day.'

'That would be absolute heaven,' I said. The shower at my apartment might be more than adequate, but the offer to luxuriate in a tub was more irresistible than the man himself. Well, almost.

We made our way up to the house and Sam let us in. He emptied his pockets and slung his bits and bobs on the hall table.

'Make yourself at home,' he said. 'I won't be long. You'll be all right changing into one of my T-shirts, won't you?' he shouted as he made his way to what I assumed was the bathroom.

'Yes,' I replied. 'Thank you.'

I stood there feeling like a fish out of water, not knowing if it was because of the anticipation of what was to come, or because I was in someone else's home—more to the point, Sam's boss's home. Yes, I'd spent a lot of time there already, but that was work… This wasn't.

I glanced around. Mum had certainly done a good job of cleaning up after everyone; there was no sign at all of our earlier catering exploits. As far as I could tell, the owners would never know anyone had been here. Knowing Sam, I doubted very much he'd have really asked permission for us to use it.

His mobile suddenly rang, almost making me jump in the process.

'Sam!' I called out, to no avail.

He obviously couldn't hear me over the sound of the running taps and I picked the handset up, wondering if I should answer it myself or just let it ring. Then again, with what the two of us were about to do, taking a call on his behalf hardly overstepped the line, did it?

Sod it. I pressed the green button.

'Hello,' I tentatively said.

'Who's that?' asked the woman on the other end.

'I'm Lydia,' I said, suspicious. 'Who's that?'

The woman's well-spoken voice relaxed. 'Oh,' she said. 'How lovely to talk to you at last.'

'Oh,' I echoed, not quite sure how to respond. This woman might know my identity, but I certainly didn't know hers.

'If you could just tell Sam we've decided to fly out a couple of days sooner than planned and that we'll be arriving late tomorrow,' she said.

I cringed, immediately wishing I hadn't answered the call. What must this woman think? As his boss, surely, she didn't condone him entertaining the likes of me at this time of night— entertaining the likes of me in her house full stop.

'Of course,' I replied, not knowing what else to say.

'And please tell him he's to make sure the house is spick and span this time,' she continued. 'I'm afraid the last time he had the place to himself it got into a bit of a state... I know he's my son and I do love him dearly, but he's way too old for *me* to be cleaning up after him.' She laughed a little. 'I suppose your mother feels the same about you when it comes to these things...'

'Sorry?' I said. 'Did you just say you're Sam's mum?'

'Yes, but please, call me Ruth.'

'So, this is your house?'

'Where else would the poor boy be staying? I'm afraid no one else would have him... Anyway, I must dash, Lydia... And by the way, I'm so looking forward to meeting you. Bye for now.'

She hung up.

I stared down at the handset, feeling like I'd just been slapped in the face. Sam wasn't looking after this place at all; his family owned it. No wonder he always seemed so at home here, it *was* his home. Well, one of them anyway, judging from what his mother had said.

Tears stung my eyes.

But why? Why would he lie to me like that?

I wasn't about to hang around for the answer. No man treats Lydia Livingston like she's an idiot. And to think what I was about to do.

I headed for the door, slamming it shut behind me.

CHAPTER TWENTY-ONE

At the deaf man's door, knock as much as you like.

I hid out of sight, too scared to move in case I made a noise. But with my heart pumping so fast even my breathing sounded loud enough to betray me and, standing there frozen to the spot, I wished he'd just get the message and go away once and for all.

'Lydia!' Sam called out. 'I know you're in there.'

He knocked again.

This was his third attempt to speak to me that morning. I had no intention of talking to that lying so and so ever again. *And I mean, ever!*

'Please,' he carried on. 'Just tell me what I've done wrong.'

What you've done wrong. I silently fumed. Like you don't already know!

I strained to hear the sound of footsteps as he eventually walked away, waiting a few more seconds until everything went quiet and I was sure he'd definitely gone.

My shoulders dropped. Phew, I could relax. Physically, if nothing else.

Mentally, I felt a mess. I'd spent hours tossing and turning, playing things over and over in my head. Thinking back to the times he'd let me believe he was some sort of odd job man when all along he was lord of the manor. The comments I'd made... I felt so foolish.

And he thinks he can come around here like he's the victim!

I sighed, realising I'd spent a lot of this so-called holiday hiding away from people for one reason or another. But at least I could console myself in the knowledge that this latest development wasn't of my own making for a change. This time, it was down to him.

I clicked the kettle on, thinking back to the very first time I clapped eyes on him, asking myself why I hadn't just listened to my instincts from the start. Then I began to think about everything that had happened these last few weeks. *So much for a bit of quiet contemplating your future.* Still, now that the wedding was out of the way I had all the time in the world to concentrate on coming up with a new direction, time to figure out where to go from here.

Knock! Knock! Knock!

Bugger! I clicked the kettle off again before the bubbling water got too loud.

'Lydia!' said Mum.

Thank goodness. It wasn't him again.

I opened the door to let her in, checking to make sure Sam wasn't lurking somewhere among the bougainvillea ready to seize his chance.

'Quick,' I said, hastily ushering her inside just in case.

'What's the matter with you?' she asked.

Now it was her turn to put the kettle on.

I busied myself getting the cups and teabags ready. 'Nothing,' I replied, getting the milk out of the fridge.

She looked me up and down. 'You could've fooled me.'

I could see she was waiting for me to say something, but I resisted. I couldn't face owning up to the fact that I'd made a fool of myself yet again.

'I must say you and Sam seemed quite the couple last night.' Never one to give up, she was obviously on a fishing expedition. But still, I stayed quiet.

'Although I did just pass him as he was getting into his car.' This was news to my ears—it meant he might now leave me alone. 'And he wasn't looking anywhere near as happy. In fact, he didn't look happy at all.' She poured the drinks and handed me my cup. 'And according to Maria, he's been in and out of their place all morning asking after you. At least that's what I think she was saying. Anything you want to talk about?'

'Not really.'

'It might help.'

I took a sip of my drink, realising I was going to have to explain at some point and I supposed now was as good a time as any. 'He lied to me, Mum.'

She took a sip of hers. 'Go on.'

I felt the beginnings of a lump in my throat and tears trying their best to well, but I wouldn't let myself cry. A man like Sam wasn't worth it.

Noticing my distress, no matter how much I tried to conceal it, Mum put her cup down. 'Come on,' she said. 'Let's forget about these and go somewhere nice. We could go to one of those places on the beach. Looks like you could do with a bit of fresh air.'

I hesitated.

'It's all right. He's not hanging around if that's what you're worried about.'

I conceded, poured my tea down the sink and grabbed my bag. 'Why not?'

We walked along the road through the village, Mum stopping every now and then to look in a window or read a restaurant menu. The sun's rays on my skin felt as wonderful as ever; it was just a shame they couldn't ease my mind in quite the same way.

'*Kalimera*!' one of the shopkeepers called out as we passed by.

'*Kalimera*,' I called back.

'This place suits you,' said Mum, as we made our way down the steps to the sands.

'You think?' I replied. After everything that had happened I couldn't be so sure.

We took our shoes off and made our way to the water's edge.

'He isn't who I thought he was, Mum,' I said, dipping my toes in the water. 'He doesn't work for the family who own that house at all, they are his family. All the stuff about him being the house-sitter was just rubbish. And to think I actually believed him...'

I stopped and closed my eyes, embarrassed. 'God, I can be such a prune when I want to be.'

'It depends how you look at it,' said Mum.

My eyes sprang open again. 'What do you mean? I've just told you his family owns that house.'

'No, you mean his parents do. So technically, when they're not around he is the house-sitter. And if you look at things that way...'

As she stared out to sea, I stared at her in disbelief, surprised she could even consider taking his side.

'I'm just saying, Lydia. That's all.'

'What? That *technically* he hasn't lied to me?'

'Well, has he?'

She turned and I followed her to one of the beachside cafés. 'What would you like?' she asked, ready to order our drinks.

'Just a coffee for me, thanks,' I said, heading for a table and plonking myself down.

I thought about Mum's words. What she was saying sort of made sense, but that didn't mean I necessarily wanted to hear it. Why couldn't he just be honest? Why keep something as simple as that to himself?

Mum came to join me.

'To begin with, maybe Sam wasn't lying,' I conceded. 'But when I assumed he was an employee, why didn't he just tell me the truth then? There is such a thing as lying by omission, you know.'

'That's the problem, Lydia. You assumed he was the hired help. And to be honest, you assume too much.'

So that made his untruths all right then, did it? I picked up the menu and began fiddling with the pages.

'You've always been the same. You take one look at a person,' Mum continued, although by now I wished she wouldn't, 'and think you've got their whole life story sewn up. You're too judgemental, Lydia, you always have been.'

Excusé moi, but when did this become about me?

'You see everything in black and white, completely ignoring the grey areas. And besides, you did lie to him first if I remember correctly,' she added—no doubt because she could.

'That was different,' I replied. Not much of a defence as defences go, but it was the best I could come up with.

'Why? Because it's you?'

Now she was just being cruel.

'No!' I said, frustrated. 'Anyway, I've already explained all that…'

I noticed a few strange looks coming our way and, smiling back, I lowered my voice.

'And look where that one little white lie got me, anyway,' I said. 'On the receiving end of blackmail, that's where!'

Mum tried to supress a giggle, not that I could see what was so funny.

'Put it this way, would you have gone out with him if he'd just plain asked?'

'No.'

'Why not?'

This was getting silly.

'Because he's not my type?'

'And how did you know? Had you ever spoken to him before?'

I knew what she was getting at; she was trying to prove her point about me being judgemental.

'At least when I did go out with him I told the truth. I told him why I'd made all that stuff up.'

'And that included telling him about the list you keep as well, I suppose?'

The waiter brought our drinks. 'Thank you,' we both said.

We got back to the matter at hand.

'Yes, it did as a matter of fact.'

'There you go then,' said Mum. 'How could he come clean after that? There you are, telling him exactly what you expect of your perfect partner, with no room for any leeway and none of it about what really maketh the man, I might add.'

Like there was any need.

'No wonder he kept quiet. He probably wanted you to get to know him the person before you tallied up what he can provide you with.'

Did I really have to keep listening to this? If mums are meant to make their kids feel better, mine was sadly lacking.

I'd heard enough.

'I can't believe you're making me sound like I'm some sort of gold digger,' I said, trying to keep the hiss out of my voice. 'I'm not!'

Tears sprang in my eyes—just what I needed while out in public.

Mum began to soften.

'Of course, you're not a gold digger, Lydia. But I can say that because I know you. Sam, on the other hand... All he could probably hear was you talking about wanting to be a kept woman.'

'Why do you keep talking about Sam's thoughts and feelings? Where am I in all this?'

'Lydia, it's just not what people expect to hear in the twenty-first century. Even you must see that.'

Of course, I saw it. I'd been on the receiving end of everyone's criticism often enough. I wiped my eyes.

'I'll tell you what else I see, Mum. What I've always seen. You saying one thing, yet doing another. You run around after Dad, Pete and Steve. Even now, when they're big and strong enough to look after themselves, you're at their beck and call...'

I paused, hoping I hadn't overstepped the mark, yet at the same time I knew it needed saying.

'Which is why it's about time you saw things from my point of view. Throughout all this, you're telling me I can do whatever I want in life. That in this day and age things are different, that I can somehow have it all. A great career, a beautiful family, and, of course, a husband who'll do his fair share every step of the way... It's a bit hypocritical, don't you think?'

'Of course, it is. Don't you think I don't know you're a product of your dad's and my making?' said Mum. 'But I have to believe that outside my front door this perfect life exists somewhere. Not for me, God only knows I've made my bed, but for you… Look, you're my daughter and I want you to have more than I've had, experience all the things I never could. And if I don't believe there's a better, fairer life for women like you, what then? Do I resign myself to the fact that nothing's changed and never will?'

I hadn't viewed things like that before and her words pulled at my heartstrings.

'But your life doesn't have to be the way it is,' I said. 'Things can change if you really want them to.'

Mum just laughed, apparently reconciled with her lot. 'You'll understand when you have children of your own, Lydia.'

Not that old chestnut.

'And anyway,' she said, suddenly perking up. 'If it wasn't for all the running around and juggling I have to do, we wouldn't have managed to get through yesterday as successfully as we did, would we?'

Now it was my turn to smile. She had a point.

'You did good, Mum,' I said. 'Thank you.'

She flushed red and shifted in her seat. 'Don't be daft. I just did what every other mother would've done under the circumstances.' She never could take a compliment.

'I doubt that very much,' I replied. 'Anyone else would've deserted me on the spot.'

'And we have your dad, Pete and the twins to thank as well,' she said. 'It goes to show how the men in this family can pull their weight when the need arises.'

'And Tammy, remember,' I said. 'We can't forget her.'

I thought back to the last few days, picturing them all peeling vegetables for hours on end, mucking in and doing their bit throughout the whole of the wedding reception, at the same time recalling how well Luke and Johnny had performed—such good behaviour having been practically unheard of up until now. And everyone was having such fun with it too. In fact, for me, it had been as much a family occasion for us Livingstons as it had for the Fatolitis.

'You see the thing is, Lydia, you've never needed our help before. At least, not like you have here this last week or so,' explained Mum. 'And because none of us wanted you to look stupid, we got stuck in and did what we could to help. So, yes, your dad might be idle in his everyday life, but when the chips are down, he's there doing his part in one way or another. And the same goes for your brothers—I think Pete has proven that. Because that's what families do, they help each other. And they don't keep score of who's doing what and when.'

I thought about what she was saying. 'I know. You're one hundred per cent right, as usual.' I leaned over and gave her the biggest hug possible. 'And thank you.'

'Which reminds me,' said Mum, when at last I let go. 'The reason I came to see you.'

'What? We've had another catering request already?'

'No...' she replied. 'Maria has invited us all for dinner tomorrow. She wants to say thank you for the wonderful job we did.'

My stomach dropped. When Mum said *all*, did that include Sam as well? Because there was no way I wanted to come face to face with that man. I would have rather had all my teeth pulled than go through that.

'Apparently, Katerina is ecstatic,' Mum said. 'As far as she's concerned, we did a far better job than the people she'd originally booked could have hoped to do, which is saying something. At least, I think that's what Maria said, she was talking more in hand gestures than actual English.'

'That's nice of her.'

'Of course, I told her we'd go. I just wanted to let you know so you don't make other arrangements.'

I fiddled with my cup.

'And will Sam be there?' I asked.

'Well, I should think so,' Mum replied. 'He did play a crucial role.'

'I'm sorry, you'll have to count me out then.'

She looked me square in the eye. 'But you have to be there, Lydia. You're not just the reason we did all this, in their eyes you're the chef, remember.'

'You know what the saddest thing about all this is, Mum?' I said. 'I'd started to forget about finding my Prince Charming, to think I could've actually been poor and whatever else it took to be with that man.'

'You should talk to him,' she suggested.

'I can't.'

'You can if you really want to.'

'Nah,' I replied. 'That's just it. I don't want to.'

Mum was worse than me for having the last word. 'As is often the case in life, Lydia,' she said, 'sometimes we don't have a choice.'

CHAPTER TWENTY-TWO

My home, my home, a little house of my own.

I wasn't really in the mood for a big get-together, but Mum had made it more than clear I had no choice *but* to attend. And like she'd said, after everything everyone had done for me, how could I even consider refusing this one simple request? She'd obviously enjoyed the hustle and bustle of the wedding and I supposed she wanted to continue with the fun.

And continue she did.

For most of the morning, I'd had to listen to her and Maria as the two of them prepared for our little gathering. Speaking in a sort of Grenglish, they'd shared cooking tips and laughed and chattered about anything and everything. The two women obviously had lots of things in common, even if language wasn't one of them. Then as the morning had gone on, they'd been joined by the rest of the Livingstons and the Fatolitis. *Well most of them.* I smiled; after all, Katerina and her new husband were well on their way to their honeymoon destination by now.

I checked my watch and gave my reflection a final quick once over. 'Not bad.'

Of course, my outfit had been carefully chosen down to the very last detail. After all, with the possibility of coming face to face with Sam, I wanted to look my absolute best, otherwise how else would he know what he was missing out on? I certainly wasn't about to tell him; in fact, I had no intention of talking to the man at all.

Time to get this show on the road. I tried and failed to quell the increasing number of butterflies fluttering around in my tummy, a task that didn't get any easier as I made my way down to the Fatolitis.

I paused at the bottom of the steps to smooth down my dress and mentally prepare. If I was going to have to do this at all, I may as well do it with a smile. And stepping forward, I glanced around ready to join in with the fun. 'Oh,' I said, somewhat surprised. 'Where is everyone?'

I must have zoned out from the background noise at some point when I was getting ready, because everything was now silent; both the Fatolitis and the Livingstons had disappeared. Apart from a lonely customer sitting in the corner, there wasn't another soul in sight. With his back to me, even he hadn't noticed me making my entrance and I just stood there, wondering what to do next.

I couldn't have got the time wrong... I checked my watch. Mum had specifically mentioned three o'clock and insisted I shouldn't be late. *But where could everyone be?*

I coughed, trying to get the guy's attention. Maybe he knew?

A tall, athletic-looking chap with short blond hair stood up and turned. 'Lydia?' he said.

'Sam...?'

He smiled, his eyes nervous yet lighting up at the same time. 'You look nice,' he said, taking in my attire.

So do you, I thought, *very nice, indeed.* Not that I was about to convey any such thoughts. What he did or didn't look like was of no consequence to me anymore.

'I hardly recognised you,' I said instead.

He ruffled his now cropped hair and rubbed his cleanly shaven chin—an action that I wouldn't have minded joining in with.

However, I immediately told myself to stop thinking like that. Regardless of his appearance, the man was still the enemy.

'So, what do you think?' he asked.

'Well, it's certainly an improvement.'

I felt a bit self-conscious being on my own with him like this. But I couldn't just turn around and walk out; the others had to be arriving soon and Mum would never forgive me if I didn't hang around to greet them.

'So why the makeover?' I asked, trying to overcome the awkwardness.

'Why do you think?' came Sam's reply.

'If I knew that, I wouldn't be asking, would I?' I thought back to my comments about him having too much hair and shrugged. 'Another one of your games, maybe?'

He slowly walked towards me. 'No games. I just wanted to show you.'

'Show me what?'

'That I was telling the truth before. That I am the man of your dreams.'

If only...

I reined myself in, refusing to let him get me all hot under the collar. Where did he think we were? In the middle of some saga?

'The man of my dreams doesn't lie to me,' I said.

The hurt in his eyes was evident, but rather than taking it on board, I took another glance around, thinking how strange the place felt being so empty.

'So where are they all?' I asked.

Now it was his turn to shrug. 'I thought you might be able to tell me.'

At last, the penny dropped.

'They're not coming, are they?' Either that or we'd purposefully been given the wrong time. 'We've been set up, haven't we?'

'It certainly appears that way, doesn't it?'

He indicated to a seat, sat down, and as I followed his lead I couldn't take my eyes off him. He looked so different. He looked so good. Not that it mattered now anyway. I told myself it was too little, too late.

Continuing to feel uneasy, I waited for him to speak first, which if experience was anything to go by he undoubtedly would.

Five... four... three... two... one...

'Lydia, I'm so sorry for any hurt I've caused you.'

I knew it.

'I just thought once you got to know me, you might start to feel the same way about me as I do about you.'

'Got to know you? Really?' I couldn't believe what I was hearing. 'So how come you told me you worked at that house then? Instead of telling me the truth?'

'But I didn't tell you that.'

Now he was just being pedantic.

'You may as well have done,' I said.

'I suppose I just wanted to find out if you could like me for me, before you started ticking your boxes off.'

My mum's words came back to haunt me.

'That's not fair!' I said.

'Isn't it?' he replied.

'No, it isn't. I was trying to be honest with you when I told you about my list. I was trying to explain why I'd made all that stuff up about being a chef... I didn't know you were going to use it against me though, did I? That you were going to laugh at me behind my back!'

'No one's been laughing at you, Lydia. Every day I've wanted to tell you the truth. To explain. Every time you asked me something about me. That day on the beach... When we went to Kos... When we kissed, especially when we kissed.'

Please don't mention the kiss...

'But you'd already made your mind up about me, so how could I then admit to being this half-wealthy doctor instead of the odd job man you'd decided I was.'

'A doctor?'

Again, I thought back. This time to when I sprained my ankle, to his enthusiasm over Hippocrates... It certainly explained a lot.

'So, what you're saying is I don't really know you at all, do I?'

'Yes, you do. You know the important stuff, you know me the person. And surely you've realised how much I care about you by now.'

'What? Like you realised how much I care about you?'

There. I'd said it! I'd admitted I had feelings for the man who now appeared momentarily stunned.

'So, what does it matter what either of us does for a living? Who cares what house we each live in? What counts is how two people feel... how we feel?'

He got up from his seat, at the same time pulling me out of mine.

'Come on, Lydia. Can't we just start again? Pretend we know absolutely nothing about each other and begin from there?'

He was so desperate I should give him another chance, give *us* another chance, I felt my defences crumbling.

'I don't know,' I said, still not quite sure.

I thought about our date at Paradise Beach and the effort he'd gone to, despite knowing full well I hadn't wanted to go out with him in the first place; about how he'd offered to support me when I'd made the decision to come clean to the Fatolitis, even though to do so would've risked his own friendship with them; and about how after Mum had stepped into the breach in order to stop me looking foolish, he'd done everything in his power to make sure Katerina's wedding was a success, not just for her but for me too.

'Please, Lydia. Let me make things up to you.'

Not for the first time, I surprised both Sam *and* myself when I reached up and kissed him.

'Okay,' I said. 'We can give it a try.'

He smiled, this time reaching down to kiss me. With his lips feeling like silk, that one kiss quickly led to another and then another... Unable to help ourselves, we were soon passionately smooching in a long, lingering and lip-locked embrace. One that I most certainly didn't want to end and neither did the butterflies flapping around in my tummy.

In fact, even when I heard footsteps and numerous chattering voices fast approaching, I had no intention of pulling away.

'Grandma! Grandma!' two little boys began to chorus. 'Aunty Lydia and Sam are kissing.'

Yes, we are, I thought. Now bugger off…

THE END

ACKNOWLEDGEMENTS

I'd like to thank the island of Kalymnos and its people for welcoming me with open arms, especially the Klonaris family who happily maintained my coffee intake during the writing of this book. Their kindness will never be forgotten.

I'd also like to thank my friend Robyn Lines for the time she spent reading and commenting on drafts of this novel. Even now, her encouragement continues to be invaluable.

And finally, a very big thank you goes to all the team at Bombshell Books. THANK YOU

25352439R00117

Printed in Poland
by Amazon Fulfillment
Poland Sp. z o.o., Wrocław